ABOUT US

By

Margaret Holbrook

Published By Empress Publishing,
Cheshire

ISBN 978-0-9929685-5-7

January 2017

Printed and bound in Great Britain
BPUK Peterborough

For Gillian
With Thanks

Also by Margaret Holbrook

Watching and other Stories,
Short stories, fiction
Cul De Sac Tales, *Humour, fiction*
Picking The Bones,
A collection of tales in the folk tradition
Hobby Horses Will Dance *Poetry*

About Us

It's so easy to judge others, but tell me, does anyone know what they will do, how they will act or react in a given situation until they have been there?
No, no-one knows. It's impossible to know and yet there are some who really do believe that sometimes there's only one course of action to be followed in any given situation.
I'm telling you now that if you believe that, you haven't faced too many of life's challenges.
I want you to read my story; to think about it and then make a decision. What would you have done? I know you'll have to make some choices, come down on one side or the other, you have to; you may see things my way or you may not.

All of this happened so many years ago and time and place are different. Everything's changed, everything except one thing, this; and this is my story.

Christine B

CONTENTS

SEPTEMBER 26th 2010

Twenty five years ago today was my wedding day, September 26th 1985; but for me the journey I was on had started the first time I met Phil. Just one look had told me he was 'the one'. From the first moment I caught sight of him I think I was hooked. He was surrounded by friends, they all seemed younger than he was, but he was the charmer, the centre of attention.

He hadn't noticed me. I was with my friends, but I was the quiet one. I was the one who just went along with the group to be part of it. Inside I knew I was only an outsider joining in. I watched him all night. By the end of the evening he still hadn't noticed me but I felt reassured that he hadn't hit on anyone else, either.

The next week at *Patches* he was there again, same group of friends, same casual air about him, and yet at the same time you knew that he was the one who stood out from the crowd. He was the one that everyone else noticed, gravitated towards. You could tell that he enjoyed all the attention but why shouldn't he? He was good-looking; he had a shock of light-brown hair that gently curled onto his jacket collar. His clothes were not chain-store; they were a few weeks' wages. Everything he did was just *right.* He could have any girl he wanted, so why should he look at me, even once? But tonight he did look at me. It was accidental. I just turned and caught his eye. He came over.

We just talked, didn't dance, didn't do anything only talk. It didn't matter, Phil Beacham was talking to me and I felt special. We arranged to meet up the following week. I wondered if he'd show, or maybe if he did would he just ignore me and stay with his mates, perhaps pretend we'd never spoken, that I didn't even know his name. Or maybe he would fake forgetfulness? Pretend that an arrangement had never been made? He did neither. He was waiting outside the club when I arrived with my friends. And from then on we were a couple. Phil and Chrissy.

That September day in 1985, the day we married; was a beautiful autumn day. A glorious day in a *'season of mists and mellow fruitfulness'*, or so one of my art teachers would have said. The one I thought was just like *Jean Brodie.* And it was, the day was all of that. They were both right, Keats and Miss Finmore.

And this was my wedding day. Oh, how I had wanted this day! My parents had really gone to town for me, their daughter. They wanted everything to be perfect, and it was. My Dad looked so proud as he escorted me to the waiting car. Mum and the bridesmaids had already left. I was worried, my stomach churning; *'Would Phil turn up?'*

Dad looked at me. I told him my thoughts.

'Come on, Chris, he'd be a fool not to,' Dad said, and he squeezed my hand. That was all the reassurance I wanted. My dad had never let me down. I knew I could trust his words. And I did. We got into the car and were driven to the church; neighbours waving as we drove by. They had seen me grow up, now they were watching as I left my home to get married.

So, everything was going to be all right, wasn't it?

And the day was perfect. Picture perfect. My special day was just what I'd dreamed it would be. At least that's what I thought.

And today, September the twenty-sixth 2010, is so special. It is my twenty-fifth wedding anniversary. Our silver wedding anniversary. Mine and Phil's, and we've come so far and are happier than we might have imagined, or could have expected, but something is spoiling today. Today won't be perfect and nothing could make it so. I feel wretched inside but I am trying to carry on, to make everyone believe in me and my false smiles.

Today isn't such a beautiful day. It is like November. Grey and drizzly. It is as light as it should ever be. As light as it will ever get. I know that it will only grow more dark as the day wears on. The sky tells its tale. There is far too much cloud about for anything else. The sun won't break through. The veil of grey mist will not clear. But Phil, nonetheless will try and make everything right, just so. He will do all of this for me, because he loves me. He says that, *'The day that is held in the heart will be as bright as any day. As bright as a summer day and as light as spring with the gold of autumn thrown in for good measure.'*

Phil handed me the paper with the words on. He'd written them down, for me to keep, a small treasure. And Phil will take care of everything. It's what he does. He's a romantic, a genuine romantic. He sorts things out and makes them good. No grey cloud could ever get in the way of anything that he wants to do. I know that. I know that he has a way of organising things to his own advantage, and I know that he wouldn't want to let me down, to make it any less special, whatever the weather. I know that Phil will make it special, for me, for us. And as it's our silver anniversary there will be something silver and beautiful for me when Phil returns from work this evening. I know there will. Twenty-five years, that's a long time to know someone, to be with someone.

Me? I've got him a special gift; a book of our journey. It shows us and our family through the last twenty-five years. It is bound in a silver case. I had a jeweller make it especially for me. I hope Phil will like it. I hope *so* much that he will. And I will find out tonight, when he comes home. We will not exchange gifts right away, no we can't, because there is something I have to do first, something that I have to tell him.

You see, what I have to tell Phil is something that will affect us all, but I can't tell him now, not yet. It will have to wait until later, until he returns from work. I will have to keep it to myself until then.

This morning Phil told me that he loved me, as he does each morning. We exchanged cards and small gifts while we were still in bed. Our ritual. Phil then brought me the roses. Long stemmed and red, another ritual; and the final part of our ritual? The special gifts we will exchange tonight, because that's the way it always is, and nothing will ever change that. No; the way Phil and I have always done things mustn't change and today should be no different.

Many times during our marriage Phil has been there to put me back on track. He sees things for what they are, and he has helped me to see things from a different point of view and not get derailed by what I saw or thought I saw, and what I wanted or thought I wanted things to be. He was the one who always kept things moving forward. Early on of course, things were never so straightforward, they couldn't be, and as my story unfolds you'll perhaps understand why; Phil wasn't always the loving, dutiful husband.

I was quiet this morning and Phil had noticed. Phil is always happy; whatever the situation he looks for the good that is going to come out of it, and he generally finds it. Me? I seem to go round searching for disasters.

I desperately tried not to think of later and told myself I was lucky to have Phil, and I was, wasn't I?

After breakfast, during which I was very quiet, Phil told me to cheer up. He smiled his quirky smile and told me that things were never so bad. He'd see me later, he said, and I wasn't to forget he'd booked dinner. How could I? He kissed me, on the forehead and then he left for work. The quirky smile solidly fixed on his still handsome face.

Everyone had been asleep when the phone rang in the early hours. I'd gone downstairs to get a drink, a glass of water. It's often that my nights are broken like this, but last night, last night was different. As I came down the stairs I realised that the phone was ringing. I wasn't expecting anything, particularly at that hour of the morning, so there and then, my thought pattern was, if it's not a wrong number, it has to be bad news. Even then, before I answered the phone, they were my thoughts. No one else was disturbed by the ringing. Maybe sometimes it's a blessing to be a heavy sleeper? And then, at that hour, how could I know that I was just minutes away from hearing Julie's voice. From hearing her muffled tears.

It all seems like a dream now as I go over Julie's words in my head, but I know it isn't. I know that everything's real, and that knowing is the hardest part. After the phone call I went into the kitchen and got myself the drink. The drink was after all, my initial reason for waking, and then I sat for a while in the kitchen, nursing the news that I had just been given. I didn't want to wake Phil and tell him because for this moment this is my news. It's mine and I need to keep it to myself. I need to grow used to it.

Anyway, whatever the reason, there was just me, only me, who was awake to take the phone call.

SEPTEMBER 26th 1985

My Mum was helping me to dress for my 'big day'. It was important to her that everything be just so. I was the youngest child and the only daughter.

We'd been on shopping expeditions to bridal boutiques and bridal stores throughout the nearby towns on a regular basis for the last few months. We'd finally hit on the 'dress'. There was lots of lace and froth, but surprisingly, I liked it.

The veil, shoes, gloves, they were all chosen with the same precise measures. Eventually, it all came together, for me. That just left Mum's outfit. That would be a complete other story on its own, we'll leave it there. I'll just say that it was all perfect on the day.

All my relatives had been invited, and friends, and friends of Mum and Dad, and Phil's family and friends. The list just seemed to keep growing and growing, but Mum and Dad didn't mind. They were doing this for me, and that was all that mattered to them. Phil hadn't any close family, just an uncle and cousin who would travel down for the wedding from Scotland, but Phil more than made up for his lack of family with all the friends that he seemed to attract.

I wasn't nervous at all, not really. I just wanted to get on with it, my wedding day. I wanted to be at the church on time. I wanted to walk up the aisle with my dad and see Phil waiting for me. That was all that I wanted. And today that dream was about to come true, about to become a reality.

Mum was struggling with my veil. My hair was long and wasn't behaving. Even the hairdresser had told me earlier in the day that my hair was *impossible.* I told Mum when I returned home, we laughed about it and then Mum said, *It's like you, then, sometimes difficult to control.* Mum then asked if Phil realised what he was taking on, with me? I laughed again. *He's known me long enough,* I thought. And what about me, what was I taking on? I didn't have a care in the world. Everything would be perfect. That much I knew. Mum was still struggling. Mrs Pickford, one of Mum's oldest neighbours was eventually called in to give help and advice. It worked. The veil was there, successfully, and invisibly pinned in place.

As the moment for Mum to leave with the bridesmaids approached, she kept looking at me and Dad. I wondered what her thoughts were; was she remembering her own wedding day? But then she came and kissed me and turned to leave for church with the bridesmaids, *like a mother hen and her chicks,* I thought. But that was Mum all over, the heart of the family. The heart of our family. As they left, my bridesmaids said that I was so lucky.

'It'll be you next, that's what they say, isn't it?' My words rang out after them.

It was just me and Dad now. He was a rock to me. He always had been. When I was a little girl he helped me with everything and anything. We went walking together, with one or other of the dogs in tow. (Growing up, we always had at least two dogs in the house). Dad knew all about the wild flowers that grew near to our home and walks with him were always a pleasure. His other great loves were books and art. Dad taught me how to draw horses. My efforts were never as good as his, but I think he liked the fact that I tried. My brothers weren't arty at all but that didn't mean there was nothing for them to do with Dad. He was also a lover of sports and football, so all three of us were well catered for when growing up. Mum, well Mum was just Mum. She kept house and cooked and baked, and taught me to do the same. Phil would be well looked after.

Thoughts were whooshing through my mind now. The time was getting near. The car would soon arrive to take me and Dad to the church. In a few minutes I would be leaving my home, this home, for one last time. The next time I came here it would be as a visitor. In a couple of hours I would be married and I would have a new home to return to. A home I would share with Phil.

Dad didn't say much to me before we left for church. There wasn't really anything to say. It was a beautiful day, and weddings rely on beautiful days, don't they? This was it, then. The moment was nearly upon us. My stomach was beginning to churn. And Dad? Dad was just doing what Dad always did. He never panicked about anything. Today he was just as calm as ever. He remained quiet, but through all this I could see that he was immensely proud. And he was proud not just of me; he was proud of all his family. I thought of Mum and Dad's wedding photo that had pride of place on the sideboard. It was the same look then. I gave a wistful smile. *Wasn't I lucky?*

And today when he walked me down the aisle, this would be his proudest moment, Dad told me this, and although it might seem gooey and sickly sweet here, written down, it wasn't like that, not at all. I was glad that it was this way. It had to be like this.

And so, within a couple of hours it was all legal, Phil and I were married. For better or for worse, in sickness and in health, to love and to cherish from this day forward. It was done. Christine Shaw had just become Mrs Phillip Beacham. The confetti was thrown, the wedding march played and the photographer took what seemed like hundreds of photographs. The happy couple left the church, and everyone smiled and cheered.

OCTOBER 1st 1985

We were on our honeymoon. We hadn't gone anywhere exotic, but I didn't mind. I just wanted to be wherever Phil was. He was mad keen on fishing, so when he announced we would be going to Scotland as there was good fishing to be had on the River Tweed until November, I didn't argue. Maybe I should have done. It's all easy to say now what should have been, but you see I was happy, and I was so much in love.

We were staying at a *fishing hotel* that Phil knew in Swinton. I know! Bells should've rung. But they didn't. Swinton was one of his haunts. He'd often visited here for fishing weekends before we were married. Today he had left the hotel early to claim his spot on the river. He liked the solitude it brought, he said. He would be back before six, before it was dark. I could spend the day as I chose. Was this it? Was this what being married was like? I thought that maybe when you were retired it got to be like this, when you'd had twenty or thirty years of being together and you needed a break, but not on your honeymoon. I wondered then whether I had just made the biggest mistake of my life, but I couldn't have done, could I? After all, didn't Phil tell me how much he loved me. And I did love him, with every fibre of my body. I did love him and I told him that, too.

He had looked at me before he left. Me in all my nuptial bridal finery and frippery. He'd looked at me and smiled, before saying,

'Enjoy yourself, there might be another fishing widow you could spend the day with.'
And then he was gone. No hug or peck on the cheek, and definitely no kissing with passion. I sat in our room and cried. This wasn't how it was meant to be. This wasn't being married. I guessed then that something was very wrong in our relationship. I'd never thought about it before, but now, well now I could see that Phil had never, never tried to get remotely close to me, never. The thought of it made me sick. What had I done? If I could have walked away 48 hours ago, well, everything would have been fine, but I hadn't known then, hadn't given it a moment's thought. I just wanted to be Mrs Phillip Beacham. That alone was going to make me happy. How wrong can you be? Phil was always surrounded by men, young men, wasn't he? And me, blindly in love and naive had never wondered why.

After about an hour of feeling sorry for myself I dressed and went to the hotel lounge for coffee. I hadn't eaten breakfast. I was too busy feeling sick and depressed about the situation and wondering what I could do about it. As much as I wanted the earth to open up and swallow me, I knew it couldn't happen. I would just have to stay and suffer the consequences, whatever they might be.

I sat in the lounge with my coffee cup for company and hoped that no one else would venture until the redness around my eyes (that I had tried in vain to camouflage) had started to subside. I would make the most of this holiday if that's all it turned out to be, and it certainly looked that way, honeymooning it seemed, was the last thing on Phil's mind.

It appeared that the rest of the *'fishing widows'* at the hotel were older than me. No one else at the hotel was on honeymoon. They were all here for the fishing. It was up to me to make the best of it, and I decided, I would.

I wondered what my parents were doing. They'd be telling all and sundry how well everything had gone. And up until Phil and me leaving the reception to head off to Scotland, everything had been fine. I was thankful for that at least, thankful that to all the guests who were there at our wedding, that we seemed to be the perfect couple. And I was glad of something else. I was glad that we hadn't stayed near home before making the journey. I wouldn't have wanted anyone to see me like this. I tried to push the thoughts that had got me down earlier on, out of the way. It couldn't be like this, no surely not? Phil wouldn't have married me if there'd ... of course he wouldn't. No. I must be wrong. When we returned home, surely things would be ok, wouldn't they? Yes. All that everything needed was a little more time.

I had, I thought, hidden myself away rather well in an alcove by the window. I was quietly flicking through a magazine and sipping my coffee when I was joined by a sprightly, but much older lady.

'Your husband gone fishing, dear?'

'Yes,' I replied.

'I often think it's a good job we've got the scenery, and of course Swinton is a good little town.'

'Yes', I offered again.

'Is this your first fishing trip?'

'Yes', I said, conscious of the fact that 'yes' was all I was contributing to the conversation.

'I've been coming here for the last ten years. I used to let him come on his own but then I thought, the children are grown and have flown the nest, why not? And even if Jack's out most days fishing, there are organised trips I can go on. So, that's what I do now, and I've got to know a good bunch of people.'

'I thought I might go for a walk around the town when I've had my coffee,' I said.

'I could join you, if you don't mind company. Give you the benefit of my experience.'

I smiled again, 'Only if you want to?'

Liz did join me and I must say I enjoyed myself. We had lunch in the town and Liz mentioned that tomorrow there would be a trip to Melrose Abbey. If I wanted to go along, there would be room.

'You'll be the youngest person on the coach, but don't let that put you off, unless of course your husband's not fishing tomorrow.'

'I think he'll be fishing every moment he can', I said.

I knew that Phil didn't seem in the slightest bit bothered about spending time with me and so I accepted.

I had always been interested in history and Melrose Abbey didn't disappoint. It was founded in 1136 by Cistercian monks and the embalmed heart of Robert the Bruce was buried in the abbey grounds, the rest of him buried in Dunfermline Abbey. The motto of the town was *'Be halde la ye hende'* or *'Keep in mind the end, your salvation'.* When I read it, it was as if it was written for me. What would be my end, my salvation?

OCTOBER 10th 1985, Wednesday

Phil and I were back home now. The honeymoon was over. Mum and Dad were pleased to see me when I called round. *What was it like, the hotel you stayed in?* Mum asked. I just answered that it was fine, and that we went on a few trips. And then Mum hugged me. I thought she wasn't going to let me go.

Before my wedding, on the day that would be my last day returning from work and going home to her and Dad, she'd said, *'I was watching you from the window, it made me sad. I'll never see you come home here again, not like this.'* I hadn't known what to say, not then. I was just looking forward to marrying Phil, and it couldn't come quickly enough. But now? As Mum hugged me, the words all came flooding back. *If only I was that girl again, if only everything could be back to normal again and I was your daughter, returning, not having to leave the family home, not having to go away with Phil, my husband. If only ...*

I hadn't brought gifts back for anyone or sent cards. I could have done. I'd plenty of time on my own in which I could've written postcards and bought souvenirs, but it would've seemed odd. What other twenty-three year old would have had time to write postcards and souvenir shop while on honeymoon? My head was spinning. I felt strange and yet I was trying in my own way to keep everything normal, to make it seem as if everything was normal, even though there was no way it could possibly be.

Mum looked at me as we walked through to the lounge. Dad gave me a wink and then went into the kitchen and put the kettle on and rattled cups and saucers in a way that he knew infuriated Mum. She called through to him.

'You can stop that, now. I'll not rise to it.' I imagined Dad smiling as he continued with the brewing up. Mum came and sat by me at the dining table.

'Are you all right Chris, you look a bit, well, not quite with us?'

'I'm fine Mum, just thinking about work on Monday. I'll have a lot of catching up to do, that's all. I just know that even though the other girls will have done their best, it won't be what I would have done. Some things will have to be done all over again. It'll take a few days before I finally get on top of everything again.'

'Well as long as you're all right our Christine. Everyone had a lovely time, you know, at your wedding. Friends have been stopping us in the street to say how much they enjoyed it. And more than one has remarked on how well you looked. And you did. Phil's a very lucky man. In fact, I shouldn't really say this, but Tony Maxwell called to the house on the Monday after your wedding. He called in he did, on his way home from work and said he thought you looked a real stunner. I think he's sorry that he let you go.'

'That was a long time ago Mum. We were both at school. Those things never last.' And as the words left my lips, I realised that I was the one who'd finished it. I was the one who'd finished the childhood sweetheart thing between Tony and me. Well look where it had got me.

Phil had already gone back in work. He loved his job. He was head of contracts at Radford's, a large electrical contractors in Hillside. When he was there he was *'just one of the boys'*. He had always made a point of this. This time last year it hadn't mattered to me, nor had it mattered to me just a month ago. I wish now that I had read more into it. I had wondered, I suppose, why he had never got close to me physically but I thought it was out of respect. I thought that he wanted to do things right. I didn't, couldn't know then how he felt about loving me. I was stupidly naive. I had been foolish, and now I was going to pay for it. No one else would be able to cancel the debt that I had got myself into. I wished that I could just leave him and start a new life somewhere else. Go off and leave someone else to clear up the mess. All that's easy to say and easy enough to do if you've no one else to think about, but I did have others I not only thought about, but cared for too, my Mother and Father, my brothers, and Phil.

SEPTEMBER 1986

We went on with our lives. It would soon be our first wedding anniversary. I had got used to Phil not coming home until late some evenings and sometimes not at all. I told my parents that he was working late, that it came with the job and wondered if they could tell that I was lying. It came to a point where they stopped asking the awkward questions and that was a huge relief to me, but you see they both liked Phil and treated him as if he were their own son. I should have been pleased about this, of course, and I would have been had ours been the marriage that everyone thought it was, but it wasn't, everything was a lie. Everything was a lie except for one thing, despite everything my love for Phil was as strong as ever. I had one wish, and it was this; I wished, hoped and prayed that come our anniversary everything would be fine. Come our anniversary maybe things would change and I really would be Mrs Phillip Beacham.

The exchanging of gifts and the roses that would become one of our rituals began that September, and to the outside world it appeared that we had the perfect marriage. Nothing else changed.

That Phil was always the perfect gentleman began to seem irksome, *'You're lucky to have him'*, was a phrase that I was sick of hearing.

Phil did treat me well in so many ways, but he wouldn't love me. And who could I tell about this sham marriage? My parents? I couldn't upset them with this. They had invested so much in me and in my *'big day'*. My brothers? Bad idea. For a start they wouldn't be able to understand. They were both married and had children, had normal relationships with their wives. They wouldn't be able to understand why I wanted to stay with Phil and they wouldn't be able to understand what the hell Phil had been playing at; marrying me when he had a boyfriend. And my friends, the girls I worked with? How do you tell your friends that your husband prefers teenage boys to you? It's not easy. I couldn't do it. I'd said for better or for worse and I had meant it. This was how it would have to be. This lifestyle was one that I was married to and the truth behind it would stay with me. No one else must ever know.

SEPTEMBER 1988

This year would see our third anniversary. We'd recently moved from our two bed semi-detached to a five bed detached. Phil had a new car. We were going from strength to strength, or so it appeared.

'Love this house, Christine, you've got it all', my Father said.

My Mother looked over her glasses at me, 'You know the old saying Christine, '*new house, new baby,*' well?'

'I'll see what Phil says when I tell him,' I laughed.

I would have liked children but Phil hadn't made any attempt at a physical relationship with me, so there was nothing doing there. What could I say? I was trapped. Sometimes I thought about divorce. I knew that I was young enough to meet someone else, but I shied away from the idea. I wasn't strong enough to talk about it to anyone, least of all Phil, and Phil had never mentioned anything about divorce either, so I suppose it was easier for us to carry on as we were. Divorce it seemed, was not an option.

But a child? Mum's words had given me something else to think about. I wouldn't know what to expect from Phil, of course, or exactly how I would broach the subject. What I did have was plenty of time to think about it. Phil was rarely in the house at all now and most of the time I ate alone. When we did eat together there were forced silences. I didn't know how to behave; it was as if we didn't really know each other anymore and yet I still felt that I loved him, and occasionally Phil told me that he loved me, too, but in spite of this I felt trapped and knew that I would remain a prisoner in this marriage unless things changed. I could see I was really no more than a 'kept woman' with none of the added extras. I was the woman who gave Phil the normality he craved but received little in return.

Phil had a regular boyfriend. He wasn't local, they'd met through work. Nick was nineteen when he and Phil first met. He had joined the company on a temporary contract, just for six months. They had hit it off straight away and carried on their relationship when Nick's contract had finished.

I don't know that any of Phil's colleagues at Radford's guessed of his lifestyle; of his liking for young adult males. Nothing had ever been said that I know of, and anyway Phil looked like any other suburban husband, so why should anyone think otherwise?

I'd been alone all day. It had given me plenty of time to think.

I'd made up my mind to talk to him, to lay my cards on the table and see what Phil would say. This, as far as I was concerned was make or break. I'd finally come to a decision.

It was ten o'clock before Phil came in. Not extremely late, but would he want to talk? I'd run through over and over in my mind the things that I wanted to say. I'd made up Phil's answers and my replies. In my head it was easy. In reality it was not. The best way, I decided, was just to dive straight in. I looked at Phil for a few moments. He seemed in fairly good humour. He didn't greet me with a kiss. Even a perfunctory peck on the cheek had all but finished a long time ago.

'Did you meet up with Nick?'

'Yes. He'll be away for a few weeks now, working in the States. So, hey Chris, I'm all yours'.

Phil smiled as he spoke. The words, those last few words he spoke made me cringe. *How had it come to this? Why had I fallen hook, line and sinker for this person? Why had I allowed myself to be used in this way?* Phil looked puzzled.

'Are you all right, Chrissy? You look worried.'

I was worried. How do you ask, how do you *tell* the man you're married to, the man you are so in love with, desperately in love with, that you want a child? Suddenly I was tongue-tied, my plan faltered and I didn't know what to say.

'I'm tired, Phil.'

'That's not it, surely?'

'No.'

'So?'

I thought I knew what I wanted to ask him but the words just wouldn't come. My rehearsal hadn't worked. I floundered on.

'Phil, sit down. We need to talk.'

'You've got me worried now.'

'You needn't be. I want to ask you something.'

Why couldn't I just say I wanted a divorce? That would have been the most straightforward thing to do, but no, I just couldn't bear to lose face. To have to admit to my family and friends that everything about Phil and I was fake; that our marriage was doomed to failure from day one was something I just couldn't do. I was in too deep now to make this startling revelation to anyone. In an odd way, I suppose, I felt safe. I knew exactly where I was with Phil, he wouldn't change. He couldn't change. But then another thought came into my head, to add to the misery I was already finding overwhelming, *I've never been unfaithful to you, Phil. You're the one who's cheated on me.*

'I'm still waiting Chrissy.'

'Mmm'. I sat down beside him on the sofa then I blurted out the words I'd been saving. The words I'd been keeping locked up inside me all day.

'I want us to have a baby. I want a child.'

Phil was quiet. Stunned I suppose. Then he looked at me and laughed.

'Chrissy, you're crazy. It wouldn't work. We're fine as we are. You've everything you need. I get you everything you need. A child would just spoil everything.'

Now I was angry. How dare he speak to me like this? What gave him the right?

'No Phil,' I began, 'a child wouldn't spoil everything. Everything's spoilt as it is. We are married but this isn't a marriage. The simplest thing would be for us to divorce but that would hurt my parents; my family who think I'm lucky to have a husband like you.'

'You must've known how it would be. You knew about my life.'

'No. Stop there, Phil. That's not how anything is or was. I thought you loved me. I loved you. I longed to be Mrs Beacham. I didn't know when I married you that I would never be your wife. I've been faithful to you. You're the one who's betrayed me, who's been unfaithful to me. You're the one taking a lover, not me. I'm just trapped here in this perfect marriage, in this perfect house, but nothing's as it seems is it? Everything about us is fake, a lie. All I am to you is a convenience. Well now I want a part of it. I want to have a child. I want to give this marriage at least a hint of normality.'

Phil looked shaken. I don't think he ever expected me to speak to him as I had.

'Chrissy you mentioned divorce. I don't want that. In my way I love you. You know that, don't you?'

'You love me as long as it suits you. You love Nick, and don't try to make it appear any different.'

'Yes. Yes I do love him. But I just imagined that when we married you'd have boyfriends. I never imagined that you'd be faithful to me. I wish now that you'd realised how it was with me. I thought I made it plain enough before we married. I thought you understood. I thought it was an agreeable arrangement for both of us.'

'I'd never felt the way I felt about you with anyone else. I was naively saving myself for you. It seems I'll be waiting a long time then, doesn't it?'

'I'm sorry Chrissy, there's nothing more to say. I can't change the way I am.'

'You're my husband. I'd like to have a child with you. I can't change my feelings, either.'

'No. Sorry Chrissy. Not a chance. If you carry on with your idea it'll have to be with somebody else.'

'So you want a divorce?'

'I didn't say that. You can have a child with somebody else, but not with me. We'll keep everything as it is and I'll support you and bring the child up as my own. I'll look after you both as best I can, but, I can't sleep with you. If you want a child you'll have to find yourself that boyfriend.'

Phil laughed again, 'I think the conversation's over now. I'm off to bed. Whatever you decide Chrissy, it's up to you.'

I stayed downstairs that night. I didn't share the marital bed. I had made my decision. Once everything had been said, it was easy. Phil and I would stay together and live as husband and wife, but, I should have my own room; a room that Phil wouldn't enter without invitation. It would be my own space. Thoughts were brimming in my head. I was excited, buzzing. For the first time in a long time I felt like *me.*

I knew that even though Phil could never love me, not really; that he would never go back on his word. He had said to me just now that he would look after me and my baby; that we would be a family, and I knew that he meant it. In that way he was dependable. Tomorrow I would start to look for my child's father, begin to make my choice, and as Phil would be paying and playing at father, the final decision of candidate would be laid squarely at his door. He didn't know that yet. I would tell him later.

When Phil came down for breakfast I was already downstairs. I had his breakfast ready.

'Hey you, didn't you come to bed last night?'

'I did.' I smiled at him.

'The covers aren't ruckled, that's all. And you know you're never still in bed, always on the move. I thought you might have fallen out with me after our conversation.'

'No. Nothing like that. We're great friends Phil, always will be I hope.'

'Oh, this sounds serious.'

'It is.'

'I'm listening.'

'Phil, I do want a baby, so as long as you don't want a divorce and I'm not bothered in that direction, then I would dearly love to have a child. I know you can't be the father but would you help me with the choice of father?'

'What if I fancy him?' he laughed.

'You might, but hopefully he won't fancy you. And, I wasn't going to go for a teenager.'

'Ouch.'

'You made me say it, Phil. I want you to be part of this, and whatever else, I know that you're a pretty good judge of character.'

'I guess I asked for it, but I do like the sound of it. I guess in a way we both win. As I said last night, in my way I do love you Chrissy, and you do give me the security I need, so yes, I'll help you. But please, only one child.'

'What if I fall in love with the father?'

'It's possible, but remember, you're lucky to have me. Isn't that what everyone says?'

I smiled. I knew I was a fool but I had got him to agree to the things I wanted, and with Phil I too had the security I needed. He was right. We would both be winners.

When Phil left for work he gave me a peck on the cheek. It was the first physical contact between us in months.

'Wait 'til I tell the blokes I'm going to be a father!'

'Wait until we know for definite,' I said, but by the time the words had left my lips, he was gone.

I no longer worked. My work was the smooth running of the home. I was a lady of leisure; one of the brigade of ladies who lunches by way of fundraising for worthy causes. Phil said it didn't seem right for me to be going out to work when he could easily support me. I was relieved not only because it meant I didn't have to face work colleagues every day, but now, well now it gave me the opportunity to search for my baby's father.

My parents were pleased of course, with the way everything seemed to be going for us. They always knew Phil was a *'good one'*. If only they knew the truth. If they ever found out what we were planning I knew that they would have both been appalled. This was not what they had planned for their daughter.

I wondered where you began to look for a father? Not a father exactly, but someone to father a child for you. Would I just pick someone up or were there agencies for this sort of thing? I needed to do some research. I decided to go to the library and read through all the classifieds. That then, would be my task for today when I returned from shopping in town.

In the afternoon as I sat trawling through papers and magazines with little success it soon became clear that the only fathers wanting or waiting to be found were those from years ago who had lost touch with their families; the fathers waiting to be reunited with long lost progeny. Not what I was looking for at all.

Escorts weren't my thing either and I was definitely steering away from IVF. To go down that route would leave my child in a sorry state, I thought. Not born entirely from love, but from a raw need and desire. This child, my child, would be loved by me, of that there was no question. But I needed love too and I wanted to be loved for myself. I wanted someone to love me; if only for a night.

I thought of the weeks before my wedding day. I was full of hope then; full of plans for my future with Phil. I smiled. *Why the hell had I been so gullible?*

And Phil's mannerisms seemed so obvious now. They shouted at me that I would never be his ideal mate. *Why hadn't I noticed back then? Could it be that I had been blinded by love?* But it wasn't only me; my parents, my family, we were all taken in. No one it seemed suspected a thing. It didn't make sense, but does anything in life ever make perfect sense? I don't know. The only conclusion I can draw is that everyone wanted to believe that everything was 'all right'. And, of course, that's what I had wanted too, wasn't it?

I returned home and gathered my thoughts while nursing a coffee cup. I had been out for most of the afternoon and was still no further forward with my project.

It was nearly half past six. Phil wouldn't be home any time soon. I stopped what I was doing and made myself a sandwich. I ate in the kitchen, alone.

I guessed that the only thing to do was to start dating again. I obviously couldn't do it here, on my home turf. I should have to go farther afield. Somewhere where the situation would be less noticeable; somewhere, where what I was going to do wouldn't seem so bizarre. Somewhere I wasn't known.

I didn't know where I should choose. I would have to go away for the weekend. That would be easy enough to arrange, and it would give Phil more of his time to spend with Nick. I thought that he would probably approve of that.

I supposed it would be like having an affair but not having to suffer any of the fallout. It would, as far as I could see, not cause any suffering to the other party. Apart from finding someone to love me, for the time it would take me to become pregnant. I wouldn't put any hold on my chosen partner. Phil had told me he would look after me financially. I didn't really have any worries. How could I lose?

Engleton where we lived was on the north coast. Northumberland, Scarborough and Bridlington were all viable weekend jaunts. By the time I went to bed, I was elated. I had fashioned some sort of a plan.

I didn't hear Phil come in, but as we were now in separate rooms it was easy to sleep undisturbed.

The next morning after Phil had left for work; I had the morning to myself and tried to decide where to go for my weekend adventure.

Phil and I had spent several weekends in Scarborough. I had an affection for the place but it couldn't be, wouldn't be, the place I would choose. The first time we stayed there, I determined to become a real wife to Phil. I was naive enough then to believe that I could change him. Well, let's face it; the first time we visited I didn't know what to expect. I thought that one day he would suddenly fall head over heels in love with me. I was eternally hopeful. Scarborough would have to be scrubbed from my list. I looked at places down the east coast and gradually ticked them off. For one reason or another they just weren't suitable. I made a cup of coffee and got out one of the maps from the bureau. I unfolded it and placed it on the table. I took a needle from my sewing basket and closed my eyes. I turned three times and eyes still closed, plunged the needle into the map. I was going to Northumberland!

I would return to the library tomorrow morning, check out Northumberland and firm up what plans I had vaguely made.

A few days later and everything was in place. I decided on a hotel that overlooked the river Coquet. It seemed quite pleasant. Not overly busy and there was always Alnwick castle as a fall back, if all else failed.

I would stay for a long weekend first. I would use my time to get used to the feel of the place. For this scheme of mine to work I should have to feel comfortable with my surroundings. I would have to check out who was there. The place had to hold some potential. I was after all, looking for the father of my child.

I booked for the following month. I knew that Phil would actually be away on business in June, so taking a break alone would not seem odd. I had to, for appearances' sake, keep everything looking normal.

The next time Phil and I met, (in the kitchen at breakfast seemed to be the norm now) I told him all the details and gave him the number for where I would be staying. He smiled, gave me a brotherly hug and wished me luck. I asked if he had mentioned anything of our plans to Nick. He said not. In a way I suppose I was glad. Phil and I still had some secrets that he did not disclose to his lover. Although what Nick would make of things when I became pregnant, I didn't know.

When I visited Mum and Dad later in the week, Mum remarked that, 'I'd a spring in my step'.

I just smiled and said, 'You think so?'

'Must be something special', she continued, 'I can always tell. You do that thing with your face. You know, makes you look just like your gran.'

'Really?' I said.

I decided there and then that Mum and Dad must never know of our plans. To them and to everyone else, we were a happily married couple. I had to be sure that it remained that way. I wasn't going to spoil the rose coloured view for them. Why should I?

The hotel was perfect. My room overlooked the river, a glorious view. I almost wished I was staying for longer than the weekend.

The next morning when I went down for breakfast it was strange. I was alone, alone in a hotel. Me. How odd it seemed for me to be anywhere without Phil. Even though our lives were pretty much separate, it still felt strange without him. After all, he was my husband.

I sat eating my breakfast, and as I did, I wondered what Phil was doing. Whatever it was, once work business was finished, I wondered whether it would include Nick. I wondered if he had gone along, discreetly of course, and whether they would be together now. Were they sitting eating breakfast together? I wondered too, if he had thought about me at all. I decided he probably had not.

I continued with my breakfast and then decided I would have some toast with my tea. There was something about hotel toast that was preferable to the home made variety. I don't know what it was. I couldn't pin point it, but it just tasted better. Maybe it was because there was no rush. You could take your time and linger over breakfast. There was no clock to watch and there was no washing up.

The rest of the day was mine to do whatever I wanted. I decided to shop, then a light lunch and back to the hotel. I was booked in for dinner at seven-thirty. Again, I would be eating alone. I promised myself that I shouldn't think of Phil or what he was doing.

I dressed carefully. I wanted to impress whoever ... I wanted to impress.

I had taken a kingfisher blue shift dress. The hem finished just above the knee. It showed my legs to advantage. I knew they were good. I wore black patent courts, (not too high a heel) and I'd some fabulous jet earrings. I think they tied everything together.

I was late getting down to the dining room. It wouldn't have to matter. I had decided to wear my rings. I was married after all and I wasn't trying to hide anything. Then I wondered if I met someone, what would they think? *Slut, playing away, poor husband!* I knew what was true, what my reasons were. *Other people could think what they liked.*

I looked around. The hotel was obviously frequented by people older than me. Retired couples, some I thought may even be celebrating an anniversary. *Really celebrating.*

I waited for my food to arrive. There were still no younger people joining the diners in the restaurant. I was the one who stood out as different. As I ate my meal, I pondered the situation. *How? Why?* These were the thoughts that were always never far away, and as hard as I tried to get rid of them from my head, they would insist on remaining.

My meal finished, I went to the lounge for coffee. I was the only person remaining. The other diners had departed immediately dinner was over. There was no chat, not with me. They were all, each and every one of them wrapped up in a world of their own. I was just a bystander. *A lot like my marriage. I was a bystander there, as well.*

I drank my coffee and went to my room. I undressed and got myself ready for bed. I listened to the radio and drifted off to sleep. Maybe tomorrow would be better.

Sunday breakfast was good. A Full English and no cooking or washing up to do, either. After breakfast I glanced at the time. It was only half past nine. Early for me to be up and ready on a Sunday, but I'd seen a church yesterday, when I'd been out shopping. I was going to go to the service.

My timing was perfect. The service didn't start until after eleven o'clock. The church was built of local stone and typical of 19th century buildings. It reminded me of the church where I had been baptised. The church where I had been married to Phil. I began to feel nervous. My stomach felt as though it had left my body and was somewhere round my knees. I couldn't go in, could I? I was about to turn away, to leave, when a voice called to me from inside,

'Surely we're not that scary, well I hope we're not, come on, come back, you might find you like us.'

'I'm only visiting the area, I can't come regularly,' I said.

'Then that's all the more reason we should make you welcome,' came the reply.

I went inside. It was a traditional service, and there was a choir, quite unusual I think, these days. Most of the parishioners were older than me, but there were younger people there. There were families with children. The church was friendly and I did enjoy the service. I stayed afterwards for coffee, and I didn't feel uneasy about it. I enjoyed it.

After my visit to church, I skipped lunch and went for a walk down by the river. It was a lovely day, warm and sunny. It was great to be out in the fresh air. I only had one more day left of my weekend. This wasn't the place to meet someone. I'd have to think again, regroup. Tomorrow I would be on my way home.

MARCH 1989

Phil told me that he and Nick were going on holiday together over Easter. He then asked me what I thought of it, although he'd already said he wouldn't be changing his mind. Whatever I thought was irrelevant; he was still going, plans had been made.

I was hurt, of course, and a little annoyed. I was always the one left alone. The one left to play house while my husband went tearing round Europe with Nick. I sniped back. More to make a point than because I wanted to hurt Phil.

'Does it matter what I think. You'll go anyway, won't you?' I said.
Phil didn't rise to the bait. I knew that he never would. It just wasn't his style.

'No, it doesn't matter what you think, and yes Nick and I are going. I suppose I'm just letting you know,' he said.

'Then go for it', I replied.

I found myself going off to Northumberland again. I stayed in the same hotel, but this time for two weeks.

I came up with an excuse for my family that Phil was going fishing with the lads from work, so I would be having a break with Linda, an old pal from schooldays. (Linda was safely out of the way in Majorca with her Spanish husband.)

My baby plans had been put on hold. I hadn't thought about it, or rather I hadn't thought about doing anything about it since my last 'weekend break'. Phil had never bothered to ask me how my search was going. I think the shine had just gone off the whole idea for the time being. I suddenly realised that like it or not, my life did revolve around Phil, and what he was doing.

When I arrived at the hotel I found it quiet. I thought it would have been busier with it being Easter. I thought there would have been more families there.

On the Sunday morning I set off for church. I recognised some of the faces from my previous visit. And the folks there were friendly, though not overpowering.

I spent my time walking by the river and shopping, and eating fantastic food in the hotel restaurant. Luckily, I have never had to a weight watcher. I manage to stay skinny whatever I eat.

I kept myself to myself at the hotel, and only spoke when someone else offered the opening of a conversation. In the evening I spent the time in my room, listening to the radio or watching TV.

On the Friday evening of the first week, as I was leaving the hotel after breakfast the receptionist said, 'It's our regular karaoke night tonight, if you're interested. It's usually very good. It starts at eight o'clock.'

I thanked her and told her that it wasn't really my thing. The young receptionist looked amazed. She was probably only five or six years my junior, but young enough for there to be a generation gap.

After dinner that evening, I could hear the sound of singing coming from the lounge bar. Intrigued, I went across and had a look. Some of the singers were pretty good. I moved forward in the crowd and wedged myself into a corner. It was standing room only. A couple got up and began singing, *'Up where we belong'*, that was pretty awful, but it didn't seem to matter, everyone applauded anyway. And strange as it may seem, I found that I was enjoying myself. After a few more acts had performed I took my leave of the proceedings and headed for the coffee lounge. I ordered a drink and sat down. There was no one else around. The coffee was good. I closed my eyes and sat for a few moments. I was actually having a good time, and I was on my own, and up until this precise moment, I hadn't even thought of Phil once. I considered it to be a result.

'Mind if I join you?'

I opened my eyes to be faced by a man with dark hair, greying at the temples, probably in his early forties.

'Feel free', I replied, feeling just a little silly. I picked up my coffee and took a sip.

'Seems like everyone else is in the karaoke', he said.

'Yes. I've just come out from there myself.'

'I've put my foot right in it then?'

'No, no,' I quickly replied.'I was just being inquisitive.'

'That's fine, then.'

As he sat down with his coffee, I glanced at his face. It was an open face, a kind face. My eyes shot down to his left hand. There were no rings. I picked up my coffee and had another sip. My rings, I realised, were on full show! Suddenly, I felt naked, as though this perfect stranger knew my life history. I hadn't planned for this, I wasn't ready, but he was *so* nice.

'A penny for them?'

I looked up and smiled.

'They're not worth it,' I said.

The next morning at breakfast, I saw him sitting alone at a table by the window. He was looking at the view. He turned as I entered the dining room and smiled.

'Care to join me?'

'I don't know, I ...' *I felt silly, like a schoolgirl.*

'Come on. You might regret it if you don't.'

I walked over and sat down. When the waitress came over I ordered a pot of tea and then went and helped myself to muesli from the buffet table. When I returned, I sat and played a little with my food. I felt obvious and uneasy. He looked at me, at my hand.

'Mrs X. I'm sorry I don't know your name. What shall I call you?'

'I could say the same thing. What is your name?'

'Marcus, Marc for short and because I prefer it.'

'Marcus, Marc, what comes next?'

'Marc Blake. And you?'

'I'm Christine, Christine Beacham.'

'I see you're married.'

'Separated', I lied. Half-lied. I thought, *we do live separate lives, so in a way, it's true.*

'I'm sorry.'

'Don't be. We've been having problems for a couple of years now. It was bound to happen eventually.'

'You're here alone?'

'Yes. Ph ... my husband is away on a fishing trip, and you Marcus?'

'Marc, please. Marcus is much too formal for a breakfast conversation.'

'Sorry, Marc,' I replied, and picked again at my muesli. I wasn't really hungry. I poured myself some tea. I could hear through all my thoughts Marc continuing the conversation. I clicked back into reality.

'You've not heard a word I've said,' Marc spoke gently as he looked at me across the table.

I looked blankly at him.

'I'm very sorry. I think I'd better go. I'm not very good company just now.'

'Ok, but if you're not busy this evening, why don't you join me for dinner, quarter to eight?'

I stood up.

'I won't take no for an answer,' he added.

I smiled. 'Then I'd better join you,' I said.

I went back to my room. I was feeling strange. Who'd ever heard of anyone being hit on at a breakfast table? It definitely wasn't planned. Suddenly, I was looking forward to the evening.

I spent most of the day in my room. I didn't want to run the risk of bumping into Marc before then. He might change his mind, and I didn't want that to happen. I wondered if he was married? Not wearing rings was no proof of anything.

At three o'clock I had booked myself in for a wash and finish at the hotel salon. I was going to have a manicure and a pedicure as well. Then all that would be left to do after that was to relax until the clock moved round to seven forty-five.

I thought all the pampering I was going through would help me; that was what it was supposed to do. It didn't seem to have much effect. I found myself feeling more and more nervous, and the time seemed to drag by so slowly. I didn't know whether to glam up a little or a lot. I didn't want to appear too eager. I dawdled around. I was skinny with the make-up; I decided to keep everything very natural.

As the time crept nearer, I began to have palpitations. I could feel my heart pounding in my chest, pattering away, as though a thousand butterflies had been let loose inside me. I began to feel sick, uneasy. *I must be a bloody fool!* I braced myself. I started to tell myself that however the evening went, my life couldn't really get any worse. I was on a road to nowhere with Phil, this meeting with Marc might take me on another journey, at least that's what I was hoping. I just hoped that my poor choice of men wasn't going to be a recurring theme. I looked at the clock. It was twenty to eight. I felt sick, I was hot, nothing about me felt right. What was I doing? I stood, stretched up and took some deep breaths. I didn't feel any better, but I couldn't turn back now, Marc would be waiting.

As I walked from the lift and down the corridor I felt terrible. My legs, my 'asset', felt like jelly. I could barely walk through to the restaurant.'*You'll be fine, you'll be fine'*, I kept repeating this mantra to myself. It wasn't helping. When I entered the restaurant I scanned round the room for Marcus. I couldn't see him. I didn't want to ask anyone, the staff, it would be too humiliating. I wanted the floor to open up and swallow me. It didn't. I looked at my watch. It was ten to eight. I'd been there nearly ten minutes. I'd been stood up! Marcus wasn't coming. I turned to go back to my room. All my effort had been in vain ... What a fool ...

'Chrissy.'

Oh no. Who knows me?

My heart filled with panic, but as I turned round, it was to see Marcus standing there.

'Chrissy, where are you going?'

'I thought you weren't coming.'

'There was a mix up with the booking. It's sorted now. Come on, I'm starving.'

The evening passed in a delightful sequence of chat, jokey interludes and amazing silences.

Then he said my name again, *'Chrissy,'* I froze, but tried to pass it off. My act mustn't have been that convincing because after a slight pause he said, 'Is something bothering you?'

'No, not really. It's just that you keep calling me Chrissy when you say my name. I told you my name was Christine but you've never used it once all evening.'

'Do you have a problem with that?'

'My husband calls me Chrissy.'

'Mmm. The *husband'*. Does it bother you then?'

'I suppose not, but it does remind me of Phil.'

'You don't want to be reminded; you'd rather it was all in the past?'

'No. It's not like that. I don't really know what I feel. It's an awkward situation to be in and I think I'd rather not talk about it at the moment.'

'You love your husband, don't you?'

'I thought I did. I was so sure I did. And he is a kind and decent man. There's no animosity between us. It just couldn't work out for us.'

'So what shall I call you?'

'Christine.'

'Just 'Christine'?'

'Why not? It is my name.'

'No. I can't settle for that. If I can't call you Chrissy, I am going to call you ...' He paused for a moment in thought and then said, 'Christa. Yes, I think that's a perfect compromise.'

'It sounds very, as though it should be someone ... classy.'

'And that's what you are, should you need reminding.'

'It's fine with me, then,' I answered, and smiled.

We had breakfast together the following day and then Marc had to leave for work. He was an architect working on a local school. A new building. It sounded fantastic. There was nothing this school wouldn't have. He told me that his job was to bring educational facilities *'into the 21st century'*. He said that children had to have the proper environment in which to learn. Getting good teaching staff is useless if they haven't got the tools at their disposal.

I thought he was lucky to have funding for such a project but he said that most of the funding was from private backers. It was the way forward, he said.

Before he left he looked at me and then smiled. He had an odd smile, rather like that of a young boy who'd done something wrong but knows that a cheeky grin will get him out of it.

'Join me for dinner this evening? It's my last night,' he said.

'Yes, I think that I might,' I answered.

I couldn't wait for the evening to arrive. I wandered round the town and had my fill of coffee shops. In the afternoon I went for a walk down by the river. There were one or two fishermen trying their hand. It was a pleasant afternoon. Just after three o'clock I walked back to the hotel. I went to my room and watched some daytime TV. I left myself plenty of time to bathe and get ready for dinner. *Tonight I wasn't nervous at all.*

I spotted Marc as soon as I walked into the restaurant. He was sitting at the same table as the previous evening.

As soon as he spotted me he stood up and came round to the other side of the table. He kissed me lightly on the cheek and helped me to my seat. I was taken aback, rather. This seemed so formal and yet it wasn't at all. Marcus was just being the perfect gentleman. He would never be anything less.

'Everything go ok today?' I asked once I was seated.

'Yeah. I think the lads on site have everything pretty much under control. It's just that someone from head office has to come out and check what's going on, on a regular basis. We have to make sure the wheels keep turning. That's where the money is, and the quicker we can have the job finished, well ... I'll not bore you, but I guess you understand'

'I think so. I suppose it's true what they say, money does makes the world go around.'

'It perhaps doesn't make the world go around but it certainly helps.'

'Will you ...' Then I paused. I wanted to ask if he would be coming back again, to this hotel, but thought better of it.

'Yes?' he asked.

'Sorry. Can't think what I was going to say. Probably because there's so much I want to say.'

'I want to ask something.'

'Sounds ominous.'

'I hope it isn't,' he said.'I've been ... well we hardly know anything about each other, but I've really enjoyed your company and so, Christa, what I want to ask you is, *'Do you come here often?'*

He laughed then carried on. 'Seriously, I just wondered will you be coming here again anytime.'

I smiled, not really knowing what to say. Marc was, or at least seemed to be a thoroughly decent man. What should I say? What could I tell him?

'Well, what do you say?' he asked.

'I don't know what to say. I wasn't expecting this. I'm here to the end of the week, but I know you're leaving today. I don't know what I can say.'

'Where do you live?'

'What?'

'You heard. Where do you live?'

'I can't tell you that. I'm sorry. I can't explain why just now but it wouldn't be ... It wouldn't be the right thing to do.'

'Right. I see.'

'I'm sorry. And no, you don't see. I'm not making myself very clear, I know, but I'm saying as much as I can at the moment. As you can appreciate, I hope, my life is in a lot of turmoil at the moment.'

'I can understand. I suppose I was being too pushy anyway. I apologise. It's just the way I am. Anyway, apology over, and to get back to my question, will you be coming here again then? I don't give up that easily you see, Christa.'

'No, you don't, do you? I can come back, I suppose. I'd have to make excuses, but ... but, where are you based, where is your home?'

'I move around a lot. My home is London. I'm originally from Kent, but at the moment it makes sense to live in the city. I ... and I do have my family home in Pinner, not that I'm there much.'

'I could perhaps meet you again. It doesn't have to be here.'

'You're difficult to pin down, for a person who's separated. You are telling me the truth, aren't you, about your husband?'

'Yes ... but then as I've just said, the whole thing is very complicated.'

'I'm sorry. But I do want to see you again. What about I give you my mobile number? You could contact me then and it wouldn't cause complications.'

'I suppose that would be all right. I'm just not sure. I didn't expect to meet ... I didn't expect to ...'

'Is everything ok?'

'Everything's fine. I've told you. It's just that my parents don't know about me and Phil and they'd be upset. We portray the happily married couple to everyone, friends and family, and we want them to go on believing it. We don't want to hurt anyone. I'm sorry, but it's my parents who would be in the middle of this. They think such a lot of Phil and if they knew anything wasn't right, well ... I worry about them.'

MAY 1989

I heard my phone when I was in the kitchen. It was early evening but Phil hadn't returned. He would be with Nick. It was the norm now. I left my phone. I didn't want to answer it. I knew it would go straight to voice mail and that I could check it later. I didn't want to know who the call was from or answer it at the moment. I also wondered if it could be a call from Marcus, but I had been disappointed on so many occasions before. And, as the time moved on, (it was now over 3 weeks since our Northumberland meeting) I little expected him to call anyway. I had begun to think that it was probably for the best. He obviously hadn't been as keen as I thought, or it could have simply been a case of out of sight out of mind, and now he was home again the few days we had together seemed a lifetime ago. I was now someone in his past.

At nine o' clock I settled down in front of the TV. I was drinking coffee from my favourite mug, (a large, conical China mug with two Persian cats languishing on it.) I opened my bag and reached for my phone and flipped it open. This time I wasn't disappointed. Marcus had left a message. I pressed the phone to my ear and listened to the voice mail over and over again. I would not delete it. He said; *'Are you in Northumberland in 2 weeks? Hope so. Marc.'*

That was it, brief and to the point, but it meant the world to me. I drank my coffee and went to bed. My mind was in a whirr. I *would* be meeting up with Marc again. I would speak to Phil in the morning. I had to get away.

I was up early the following morning. I hadn't had a good night's sleep, how could I? My thoughts all night, the ones that had insisted on keeping me awake, were of Marc, and our next meeting. The lack of sleep however, didn't seem to matter. I felt fresh and rested as though I'd slept for days rather than hours. And being early had another benefit; I didn't want Phil to have left before I had chance to speak to him. When he did come down to breakfast, he too was looking quite dapper. He'd obviously had a good night with Nick, one way or another.

'Oh, morning Chrissy. I didn't expect you to be up so early, everything all right?'

'Fine, but we need to talk. I need to talk to you now before you leave for work, so get yourself sorted and sit down. I've made you tea.'

'Thanks'.

When Phil sat down I began. I told him that I'd met someone in Northumberland and that we wanted to meet up again. He could be the one, *'the father'*, I blurted out.

Phil began to laugh.

'Chrissy. I never thought you'd take the whole thing seriously. I thought that if I went along with you, with your plan, well I thought that you'd have some fun making 'your' plans and ... and, well I never thought you'd really want to go ahead with it. I didn't really think that you'd go ahead and meet someone ... not really. I thought you'd just get the whole silly business out of your system and we'd get back to normal.'

'What?' I said, 'So you didn't mean a word that you said to me. None of it was true. You've lied to me, strung me along just as you did when you asked me to marry you. You obviously have never thought much of me. Not much at all.'

'Look, calm down Chrissy. I didn't think you really meant it, that's all. And you know what you mean to me, you're my wife after all. So, I apologise Chrissy. If it's what you want, the baby thing, go for it. I'll not stop you. So, tell me now, I want to get it clear in my mind. You're meeting up with this man again?'

'I'd like to. He seems nice, genuine.'

'What time were you thinking of?'

'There's a bank holiday at the end of the month. I thought I could go Saturday and come back Monday.'

'Do what you feel, Chrissy. I'm sure it will be fine.'

'But what about my parents? I don't want them to find out. I want everything to seem ok. They think a lot of you and I don't want to let them down. You will go along with me won't you? I don't want to lose you either. You see Phil, I want your assurance that you will stand by me, be there for me as I've always been for you.'

'I'll cover for you if they drop by. I can be discreet.'

'Thanks'. And it's not a 'baby thing', don't use that expression please. I'm doing this because I want us to have a child.'

I took Phil's hand and held it for a second. I did still love this man. He'd single-handedly caused so much havoc in my life, and yet, I did still love him. He smiled at me and said he had to go, he didn't want to be late, but that I was to go ahead and sort out my 'mini break'.

As soon as Phil had left I phoned the hotel and made a reservation for the twenty-seventh. I managed to get the room I had been in previously. I felt sure everything was fated to be. I then sent a voice mail message to Marc, telling him that I would be arriving in Northumberland on the Saturday, around two o'clock.

When I arrived at the hotel, the weather was fine and dry but blustery. I was almost blown away a couple of times and felt an absolute wreck when I reached the hotel reception. The receptionist actually remembered my name. That made me feel brighter, anyway! I went straight up to my room and freshened up. I didn't know whether Marc had arrived or not. I didn't dare ask. As soon as I had unpacked I sent him another message, 'I'm here. C.'

I stayed in my room until four o'clock and then went down for coffee. I hadn't had a reply from Marc. As I passed reception, the attendant beckoned me over.

'We've had a message from your husband, Mrs Beacham. I'll just get it for you.'

I must have gone pale as when the young woman returned, she said, 'I don't think it's anything to be concerned about.'

I muttered my thanks and went and sat down on a chair in the corner of the lobby. I opened the envelope and read, 'Christa, *Christa? It must be from Marc. I had nothing to concern myself with, regarding Phil, then.* My countenance at once changed, *things were fine.* I carried on reading.

'Join me for coffee, if you like. Marc.'

I smiled at the receptionist.

'He wanted to surprise you, I think. He's in the coffee lounge.'

Marc was grinning from ear to ear as I walked through the lounge door.

'You certainly take your time getting ready, Mrs Beacham. I'd almost given up hope of you ever leaving your room.'

I hurried to the seat next to Marc and sat down.

'What do you mean saying you're my husband? Won't the staff think that it's unusual that our names are different?'

'I'm not booked in here, not yet. I'm at a hotel down the road. We'll have dinner there tonight. I hope you'll join me anyway, as I've booked a table for two.'

'I thought you were staying here. I'm sorry Marc, I'm confused, what's going on?'

'Nothing. I just thought it better to do it the way I have, that's all. And, I mentioned at the reception that I was working in the area, which is perfectly true, and I happen to be staying in a different hotel, again true and that you've come up to visit your sister, she's had an accident while on holiday, you're visiting, and that's nearly true. And, I thought we should have dinner together and I wanted to surprise you. The young one, Libby, she thought it was *'very romantic'*.'

'I'm sure she did.' And then he surprised me a little more, he leant over to me and kissed me, very briefly on the cheek.

'Glad you could come, Mrs Beacham.'

'Didn't the receptionist remember you as Mr Blake? I'd be surprised if she didn't. They have a good memory for names and faces, hotel staff.'

'And they're also used to being the souls of discretion. You've nothing to worry about, Mrs Beacham, believe me.'

The waitress arrived at that minute with the coffee. I was dumbstruck, again. I liked Marc but I felt as though I was stringing him along, even though I wanted to be here, I was here for one reason and one reason only.

I enjoyed Marc's company; I knew this from the last time we'd met. I knew that I had to tell him the truth, not just give him the glimpses that I felt were enough to explain my behaviour. I had to tell him everything, and then it would be up to him. Where it would leave me, I didn't know. But I knew I had to be honest with him. I sat very quietly for the next few minutes, Marc eventually breaking the silence.

'Mrs Beacham, you are distinctly quiet, please speak to me!'

'That's because I don't know where to start.'

'You're a puzzle. Come on, I won't bite.'

'Who are you? I want to know.' I paused and then carried on, 'And then there's more I need to tell you, more you should know about me, and I will tell you, but not here. There are too many other *'ears'*. Let's have our coffee and go for a walk.'

Marc was stunned by all my talk, but agreed. We finished the coffee and went out into the fresh May air. It was still quite blustery.

'Where do you want to go?' he asked. 'You're not a spy are you, from a former Soviet Bloc country hoping to take over Northumberland?'

'Don't be so silly. I need to talk to you. When I'm here I usually walk down by the river. It's pleasant down there and some parts are quite secluded. We can talk and not be disturbed.'

Marc followed my lead and we went down on the river path. There were few people about. Not enough to bother us or notice us. We sat down on a bench and watched as the ducks bobbed up and down in the river. Fluffy brown ducklings were trying to keep up with the flow of the water and still keep in sight of their mother. It was all quite charming. I turned and looked at Marc.

'I don't really know where to start but there are a few things I need to know. I know your name, and that you're working on the school and that you live in London and are originally from Kent, but that's it. I want to know more.'

'We've only recently met, Christa. I think you know enough to be going on with.'

'I'm sorry. But I need to ask, are you married?'

'No, I'm widowed. My wife died two years ago.'

'I'm sorry.'

'It's all right. I'll tell you more in the future.'

'The future?' I laughed.'I don't think that's to be talked about yet. I have so much to tell you.'

'I'm not going anywhere.'

We sat for an age, by the river. I was surprised that he didn't just get up and go when he heard my story but he stayed.

'You don't do things by halves, do you?' he said.

'I don't do things much at all. What do you think? Will you enjoy my company this weekend after what I've told you?'

'I've booked us in for dinner at my hotel at seven-thirty, I'm not missing that. Let's just carry on as we'd planned and see where it leads us. What do you say?'

'Ok.' I replied.

JULY 1989

I had nothing to worry about. Marc wanted to carry on seeing me. If I had told him the whole truth, I was afraid he might change his mind, or back off, so I didn't tell him everything. I kept back the one thing that was probably the most important of all. I didn't tell him about how desperate I was for a child. What he would think of me should I tell him, I couldn't bear to think.

Marc, for his part, had told me that he thought I was foolish to stay with Phil, a man who took a lover, and was so blatant about it. He wasn't so put off by the fact that the lover was a man; it was just all the lies that Phil and I were weaving for ourselves. The lies that kept the rest of our family and friends sweet, that was what really bothered Marc, that was what he couldn't come to terms with. He told me that he thought by trying to fool everyone else, we were both only fooling ourselves. He said it would be best for me to divorce Phil and make a fresh start, with him. I told him I couldn't do that. I had to stay with Phil. I had to stay in my marriage. Marc asked if my reason for that was that I was still in love with Phil. *He seemed to know me better than I knew myself.* Of course I was in love with Phil, although the reasoning behind it would probably need a psychologist to figure out. I knew that there would always be a part of me that would never be able to give up on Phil, but was this so wrong? And of course, I had to consider my parents. They liked Phil. They thought we were the perfect couple. How could I let them down by telling them that my whole life for the last three years was just a sham?

I arranged to meet up with Marc again in August. He would be in London and it was easy enough for me to get there. I would drive over on the Sunday; the day before the bank holiday and the day after my birthday. I knew my birthday would be special and taken care of. Phil always made sure of that. Marc didn't ask me to stay with him in his home, which I thought odd, but insisted I stay in a hotel. I didn't question him about it. I went along with it. I just wanted to see him again. So, everything was sorted, my weekend was planned and to his credit Phil was fine about it all. I'd shown him a couple of photos of Marc. Phil said he seemed 'An ok bloke', and then added, 'and don't worry Chrissy, *he's not my type'*.

'*No*', I thought, *'He's too old'*.

AUGUST 26th 1989

Today is my birthday. Phil is the absolute gentleman, as usual. Today I will be spoiled. Today Phil will make it his job to 'entertain' me. He does plan perfect days, right down to the last detail. He brought me breakfast in bed at quarter to eight. Juice, cereal, toast and marmalade, and afterwards – champagne! But that's Phil. After breakfast, (our first together for months) we had coffee while we sat in the conservatory and watched the world go by. When he gave me my gift, Phil took my hand and gently squeezed it. My eyes pricked with tears. This was all so *right*, except it never would be, would it? I couldn't hide the emotion that was welling up inside me. I *did* love him.

'Hey, don't get weepy. It's your birthday,' he said.

'I know, and as always, it's perfect. Thank you Phil.'

I looked down at the small box and when I opened it, the tears really did flow.

'Chrissy, it's your birthday. Your day to be happy. Come on, don't you like it?'

How could I not like it? It was a ring with six small opals and diamonds. Opals were not my birth stone. I wondered if it was unlucky? I didn't say anything. Then I looked at him and he was grinning. He took my hand again and kissed me briefly on the forehead.

'Happy birthday, Chrissy'.

If things were different I know he would really love me. I know he would.

We drove to a country pub for lunch, and then we went for a walk. We used to go for walks often in the early days of our marriage, in the days when I still clung on to the belief that Phil would come to love me.

Phil got a kick from the outdoor life. Just being in the countryside and the feeling it gave him was like a fix. I enjoyed it too, and Phil, whatever our differences, was always, always good company.

And today it was good being *'just us'*. It felt really special. I wondered if I could make him fall for me, forget Nick, and remember that I was his wife.

That evening we went into town, to the theatre. I had been wanting to see a play by Marco Carmoletti, a comedy. We had missed it the last time it toured. I was pleased that Phil had remembered. But that's what he did, wasn't it? He remembered every word that had passed between us, remembered where we were when we did certain things. He put a lot of thought into everything he did for me. He'd remembered what I'd said about the play. He hadn't forgotten. That must mean something, mustn't it?

That night, when we arrived home, Phil was very attentive. I wondered if he would be mine, completely, as I had wanted him to be from the day I married him. I shouldn't have bothered giving my longings a second thought. It wasn't to be, not tonight and probably not ever. After what had been a perfect day we went to bed in our separate rooms. In the morning, things were back to their usual routine.

AUGUST BANK HOLIDAY 1989

Marc met me at the hotel. I saw him in the car park as I pulled up. He'd reserved a room in the name of Mr and Mrs Blake. We checked in and went up to the room in the lift. My stomach was in knots. It was only a quarter past one; we had a whole afternoon in front of us and then dinner.

I was giddy with the anticipation, just thinking about the evening ahead made my stomach do cartwheels.

We went out into the city and had some lunch and then filled up the time doing ordinary, 'touristy' things; a little sight-seeing and a whistle stop tour of the art galleries and museums. The time went so quickly.

By the time we arrived back at the hotel it was about six o'clock. When we reached our room I was feeling nervous again. Perhaps I was even more nervous than I had been earlier in the day. I was so unsure about everything. I hoped that what I was doing here, with this man, was the right thing.

Marc said that I seemed quiet. He didn't know the half of it. I was quietly having all kinds of panic. What could I say? I took deep breaths and told myself to, *'Stay calm, stay calm.'*

Marc looked across at me and then said, 'Mrs Blake, it suits you.'

'Don't say that. It's not good. It makes light of the whole situation, and you know what I said about Phil ... and ... and I meant it. *Time to change the subject.* What happened to your wife, how did she die?' I asked. Then wishing immediately the words would reverse straight back into my mouth.

'A car accident. She was driving, swerved to avoid a dog and ran into a lamp post. I escaped with scratches but Linzi died. They said it was instant.'

'I'm sorry. I shouldn't have just blurted that out.'

'It doesn't matter now, forget it. You're here, that's all that matters to me, now; and *Mrs Blake*, and before you interrupt, I'm saying it because I like it. I'm not making light of anything. This situation is far too serious to make light of. And I know what you've told me, about you and Phil and how you don't want to upset your mum and dad and family and friends. The list seems positively endless, but, the offer's there, should you ever change your mind. Now to carry on, Mrs Blake, what do you have to say for yourself coming up to this hotel room with me? Come on, answer now.'

'Don't tease me Marc. If you knew how I felt, you wouldn't tease. I'm actually scared to death.'

'Of me?'

'Of the situation. I feel ... it feels as though I'm cheating.'

Marc didn't say anything. He looked at me and then he kissed me, and I kissed him. I was twenty-six years old and this was the first time I had really been kissed. I suddenly lost my appetite for dinner, as did Marc. Marc closed the blinds and helped me undress. It seemed natural, right. I slipped into bed. The bed sheet felt cold against my skin and I shivered. I watched Marc for a long second as he silently undressed. The next second I felt Marc in the bed next to me. He was warm and he was next to me. And then Marc did what Phil had never wanted to do, never made any effort to do, he made love with me. It was more than I had ever imagined. There was just one thing missing, though. Marc didn't speak any words of love to me, although I hoped there was some love there; after all, hadn't he just said earlier that he wanted me to be Mrs Blake? I hoped he wasn't fooling, just stringing me along. I didn't want that. I was quiet, thinking about what had just happened.

Marc looked at me.'What's the big point of anguish?' he said.'I expected something from you, not just silence.' There was a pause, and then he asked, 'Are you all right Christa?'

'Yes', was all I could say.

We lay together for a while. Marc had his arms around me. It was good to feel protected this way. I was content to just lie where I was, comfortable and secure and knowing that my life had changed forever.

I'd never said that I loved him, had I? In fact, I'd more or less told him the complete opposite,

saying that I was in love with Phil. I felt as though I'd got everything I'd ever wanted now, so why didn't it feel so good?
Maybe I would come to love him. Maybe one day my feelings for Phil would change, and I wouldn't love him or feel so tied to him anymore. Maybe one day I could be Mrs Blake? The thoughts were running through my head like water down a stream. They became a torrent of thoughts that wouldn't stop.

But here, now, as I lay with Marc, I hoped that one day those words of love might come.
Marc kissed me on the forehead and then got out of bed, and checked his phone.

'Were you expecting a message?' I asked.

'Yes and no. I thought that there might be something from my sister but there's nothing, so that's fine.'

'Your sister?'

'She keeps an eye on my house while I'm away, that's all.'

'I see.'

'You don't, and I'm not about to go into anything now, so don't ask.'

'Fine,' I said and smiled. I wanted an end to this particular conversation. It was obviously going nowhere.

'We haven't eaten, yet, and I cancelled the table in the restaurant before we got back to the hotel,' he said.

'You did?'

'Yes. I thought things might happen, and they did.'

'Presumptious.'

'Intuitous.'

'I see,' I said, and smiled.

'There's room service til nine, after that it's just sandwiches from the kitchen.'

'What time is it now?' I asked.

'Eight-thirty. We'll have to make a decision.'

'Are you very hungry?'

'Not really,' he said, and got back into bed.

Three more weekend meetings came and went. Each time I met with Marc it was special. He kept up his *Mrs Blake* routine, and I must say that I was growing to like it. And I did like him. But who wouldn't? He was just about perfect and by the time of our last meeting that year, (Christmas was fast approaching) I think I was falling for him. Marc made me happy. It was a wonderful discovery to make and I felt that at last, everything was right with my life. The only little blot on the landscape? I still wasn't pregnant. I began to wonder whether Marc might have had a vasectomy. Maybe he and Linzi hadn't wanted children? If this was the case, I was certainly making hay in the wrong field. I couldn't risk falling too much for this man and then have to start the whole thing all over again with somebody else, look for another potential father. The thought of it filled me with feelings of depression and I decided to stop the whole thing there. Not go over it any more. I'd got Christmas to look forward to and Christmas was a time for families. And Christmas at the Beacham house was spectacular. Phil always enjoyed Christmas time. It was one of his favourite times of the year and we celebrated in style. He loved entertaining and my family were always top of the list. He loved them. That meant all the family spending Christmas day with us. That included my brothers, Ken and Bill and their wives, Sheila and Carol. Between them they had five children so it was a busy affair, but everyone loved it. Phil was the consummate host. He revelled in it. He began planning the light display at the beginning of November. The outside of our house was one great big winter wonderland. We used to see people pull up in their cars, get their children out of the back and then come and gaze at our display. At Christmas we were one of the best free shows in town.

And the day itself? Nobody was allowed to nod off in front of the television. Everybody had to take part in the festivities. Everybody had a party piece to do. My brother Ken, spent most of the year thinking about what he would do, and then ended up as always doing an impression of *Tommy Cooper.'* You know you like it', he said, and we did, particularly Mum.

When Christmas arrived, I had other thoughts on my mind, I wasn't just thinking of making the day enjoyable for everyone; I kept thinking about Marc and about what he would be doing. How he would be spending the Christmas holiday. I didn't know about his family. I'd tried to ask but I never seemed to get a reply. I knew he had a sister, Julie, who house-sat for him, and that she had a son. That was as far as it went. Try and dig any deeper and he went very tight-lipped. He was a puzzle, an enigma, and though I knew that I shouldn't be feeling the way I did, I couldn't help thinking about him. For now, I had to be content with the memories of our meetings. They would have to get me through to the New Year, when we would be able to meet up again.

Thinking like this, about Marc, made me realise that what I had with Phil, what I'd thought I had with him perhaps wasn't love at all. It was a friendship. Even when we were courting, we were only friends. He'd known it all along. It had taken me a lot longer to realise the truth. How did I know this? With Marc, the merest touch of his skin and I would tremble inside. I only had to see him and I felt a glow. I began to think back. Had I ever felt this with Phil? To be honest it was so long since Phil and I had done anything together that my memory was hazy. I just couldn't remember, and yet a part of me still wished we were more than the *good friends* we seemed to be. The only time there was any physical contact between us was anniversaries and birthdays, or family events where we had to *look right.* Family events like today, like Christmas. Today we were the happy couple everyone believed us to be. And we both played the part to our advantage. We'd had a lot of practise.

So even though my heart was in another place I did my best to hide it. I smiled and hugged and kissed and cooked dinner. Phil *entertained,* everybody. My nephews and nieces enjoyed themselves, they always did. They loved their Uncle Phil, and he had a never ending stock of games, (and none of them boxed or bought), with which to entertain them.

By the time the day was at its end, all of us, children included, were tired out and ready for our beds. I wondered how Mum and Dad coped with it all. The idea of coming round to your children for Christmas was to make it easier for you as you got older. The Christmas days that Phil organised gave no one any chance of a quiet or easy time.

On Boxing Day it was more or less a rerun of the previous day, but this time it was 'open house' for friends as well. Phil, always the 'people person' loved the fact that he got the chance to do it all again. I sometimes wonder how we kept going, but we did.

Towards the end of the evening Mum followed me into the kitchen. She was carrying unused cutlery and plates.

'I'll just put these back, no point in making washing up.'

I knew these words were an excuse, an excuse to get me on my own and talk to me. After a few minutes she sat down at the kitchen table and watched as I busied myself at the sink, rinsed plates and replaced them into the dishwasher.

'Everything all right?' she asked.

Playing dumb, I said, 'What do you mean?'

'Well, you and Phil, you seem a little distant. You're not your usual selves. You've not had a falling out have you?'

'No, nothing like that. Can you keep a secret, Mum? You've not to tell anyone, not a soul, not even Dad.'

''Course I can. I knew there was something.'

'It's nothing bad, if that's what you're thinking. It's ...'

I went over and closed the kitchen door. Phil caught sight of me and smiled. I smiled back, then my back against the door, (to prevent unwanted interruptions), I whispered, 'We're trying for a family, that's all, but, well, it's not all plain sailing.'

Mum got up, her face beaming. She came over to me and hugged me.

'Oh, I'm so glad. I'm thankful there's no nastiness. I wouldn't want that, you're so lucky Christine.'

That was all it needed to keep Mum happy. The words that told her she might be going to be a grandparent, again. So, with her duty done, she went back into the lounge, still with a slight smile on her face. I knew Mum wouldn't give away any secrets. She wasn't that kind of person. You could tell Mum anything and be secure in the knowledge that it wouldn't go any further, not even as far as Dad. Her word was true and dependable. I knew I had nothing to worry about. She would be fine now for at least another few weeks, when she might begin asking me how things were going. I went back to stacking plates. It made me wonder though, Mum had noticed a distance between me and Phil. A distance that we were trying so hard to hide, so, if Mum had noticed, had anyone else, and were they just being polite in our company?

Phil came into the kitchen. 'What's up with your Mum? She's just come up to me and squeezed my arm and said, *'I'm so glad'*, and then winked. I thought I'd best come and have a word with you. She's all right, isn't she?'

'Never better,' I said. I've told her that we're trying for a family.'

Phil put his arm around me, 'I'll not let you down Chrissy, never.'

I looked at him, and I knew he wouldn't. I believed this man. He wasn't my lover, but he was one of my best friends.

JULY 1990

Marc and I continued to meet, usually at least twice a month. When we could, we would meet more often. Phil was with Nick. It wasn't like I was leaving him alone, abandoned. The one thing I was conscious of, *did my family suspect anything?* If they did, they never said anything, and Phil was as good as his word and would always provide me with a plausible alibi. Marc would meet me in London, and we would assume our role as Mr and Mrs Blake, at our hotel. I wondered if any of the hotel staff really knew the way it was between us? If they did, and I suspect they did, they never let it show, but then I'm sure they'd seen it all before anyway. It wasn't exactly new, was it? On my part, I had become used to it. It was just a way of life. And while I was with Marc, well my life with Phil didn't seem to matter. Phil and I were after all living separate lives, and yet for the success of this venture, I relied on Phil implicitly. For all that separated us, there was a link that neither of us could break.

I lived between my meetings with Marc by waiting for the next and was convinced that I was falling in love with him, (which was easy enough to do) but I knew that I was still in love with Phil in a strange, platonic way. I knew it was silly, but I was trapped in a web of my own making and I didn't want to escape.

The only cloud on what seemed like an otherwise bright horizon was that I wasn't yet pregnant. Mum had dropped the odd hint or two that I should go and see the doctor, '*there's all kinds of things they can do now to help nature on its way*,' she had said on more than one occasion. I brushed her helpful comments aside and gave my stock reply, 'We'll see, we're giving it time.'

I only wished I could speak to Marc about it, but I couldn't. I had to keep quiet. He'd no idea that the only reason I went with him in the first place was to fulfil my desire for a child, and I wondered if he, in his other life with Linzi, well ... I wondered if they had ever wanted children? I desperately wanted to broach the subject with him. I would have to think of a way.

When Marc and I next met, Phil and Nick were in America for two weeks. It was yet another of their 'business' trips. Mum said she couldn't understand Phil having to make all these foreign trips and me being on my own so much. She said that she didn't think it was good for me, and she didn't care for London, either. She thought it was a *'Mixed up place'*. She was probably correct on all counts. Whatever Mum said was never far from the truth.

Her words made me think. What was I doing? I didn't seem to belong anywhere, not any more.

When we stayed in London it was always wonderful, really wonderful and I looked forward to these meetings with Marc so much, and yet this time I still had the words from my Mum ringing in my ears. It was as if she was there, urging me to have caution, to take care in my actions.

'You're quiet, Christa, come on, what's bothering you?'

'Nothing, just thinking about Phil and Nick. I'm sorry. I probably don't make for good company do I?'

'You're my good company always, don't forget, will you?'

I smiled at Marc, unlinked my hand from his and put my arm around his waist, drawing him to me. 'Thank you,' I said.

Back in our hotel room, I still hadn't managed to lift my spirit, not completely and it made me think of something that had passed between us a couple of nights ago. An event so recent, that I could still almost touch it, hold it in my hands.

It was on the first evening in the hotel as we were going down to the restaurant, Marc took my hand and held it tightly, almost to the point that he was hurting me. He pulled me to the wall of the corridor.

'What are you doing?' I asked, a hint of urgency in my voice. Marc loosened his grasp, and looked at me apologetically.

'I'm sorry. I didn't mean to hold you so tightly. This is supposed to be special. I'm asking you to marry me. I'm asking you once and for all to leave your husband and be my wife. I want you to become Mrs Blake, officially.' And then he kissed me.

When I'd recovered my breath, he stood back and looked at me, 'Well, what do you say?'

'I can't. I'm sorry, Marc.'

It wasn't the answer he'd wanted. We walked in silence to the restaurant. Marc never mentioned the proposal again. We ordered our food and the silence between us remained unbroken. It was awful. I wanted Marc to speak to me. I wanted, in my own way to try and put things right. I imagined that I could have lost him, forever, and what that would feel like. When the food finally arrived, my appetite had all but gone. Marc looked at me across the table. After a few moments he said, 'You're not on a diet, are you? You've hardly touched your food.'

'I'm not very hungry,' I said.

'I see.'

I looked at him. I had to say something. I couldn't go on like this,

'Marc, I need to ask you something. Why am I never invited to your home? Every time I come to London we meet in a hotel. It's so seedy. It makes me feel cheap. I feel as though I'm being used, I don't think I can carry on like this.'

'I must say, calling this seedy is a fine start to a conversation from the woman who has just turned down a marriage proposal from a man who loves her and wants to be with her. You've turned me down for your husband who has no idea about you. Who can't possibly love you or he'd be here with you now instead of being in America with Nick.'

'That's a terrible thing to say.'

'It might be, but it's the truth. And what we're doing isn't seedy. Or at least I didn't think it was. You make of it what you will.'

'You've said you love me. Do you mean it? You're not just stringing me along?'

'I would never do that. I want to marry you Christa. Just you remember that.'

'The hotel staff don't say anything, but I bet they know. Can't you see none of this is real? We're living out lives that aren't truly ours. I think it's because we've never been truthful with each other. You're holding back from me Marc, why?'

'You're being very deep tonight Christa. I've nothing to hide, honestly.'

'Then why don't I ever meet you at your home, why? Marc; you say you love me but do you, really? Do you have any real feelings for me?'

'I've just asked you to marry me. Do you want me to spell it out any more plainly than that? If you do, you'll have to tell me what to do, because I can't think of anything else.'

'Just tell me why I'm never allowed near your home?

'Steady on Christa, this is becoming an inquisition,' Marc looked at me and smiled.

'Don't make light of it Marc. I'm trying to be serious.'

'You're right. We could meet at my home. You could stay there when you come to London. It would be a lot easier in some ways. Next time we meet, don't drive down, take the train and I'll pick you up at the station and drive you out to Pinner, I promise. Now the tricky bit. Let me see ... Mmm? Yes, I love you.'

Marc and I didn't meet up again until the end of July. It suited us. There were family problems piling up for me and it was making a getaway difficult.

I'd gleaned from Phil that he was starting to have problems with Nick. I wondered whether it would all end between Phil and Nick or whether it would just resolve itself and they would be all lovey-dovey in another week or two. Whichever way it was going, Phil was very cut up about it and although he said that he liked having me around, I thought that it might be better for the two of them to go away and sort out their differences. And there were other problems, too. Why is it that things seem to happen all at once? My dad started to be ill and I was spending a lot of time helping Mum. I cooked and cleaned and did their shopping for them. My father seemed as if he was losing the will to live. Everything was a trial. And doctors didn't seem to be able to offer any reassurance. There seemed to be nothing they could do. They hadn't any answers for what was making him so ill. He had all the tests known to man: blood tests, x-rays, scans. He was even kept in hospital for a couple of nights for observation. No one was any the wiser when they'd finished. Mum thought they were experimenting on him.

'That's why they don't tell you anything after all the tests they've done,' she said.

'They do tell you something, Mum. They keep telling us they don't know why he's so ill. There's no reason for it.'

'I wish I could see his notes. That might give something away,' she said.

You can look at them if you really want to. It's your right. We just have to ask.'

That quietened Mum. I could see she was giving it some thought. I also knew that that was where that particular conversation would end. The next week when I called round to help out, Mum and Dad were busy chatting. Dad was brighter than I had seen him for weeks, and I said so. 'I'm sorry our Christine, but I've just told your Dad your news. I thought it would cheer him up, and it has, it's worked wonders.'

'What news is that?'

'Don't be silly, Christine. The news about the baby'.

I smiled. This wasn't like Mum. And besides, *there was no sign of that yet.*

My announcement of another trip to London was greeted with dismay.

'Who'll help me with Dad?' Mum questioned.

'I'm sure Ken and Bill will come over. Sheila and Carol will help, and it'll cheer Dad up to see the grandchildren, plus, I'm only away for three nights.'

'The children are too noisy. They'll upset him.'

'Dad would never say that.'

'He does. He's always better when they've gone.'

'You just said he would pick up when his new grandchild arrived, you can't have it both ways.'

'Don't be lippy, Christine. This is my house.'

Mum still had a way of making feel ten years old and knowing when it was time to bite my tongue. The years may have come and gone but I was still her child, her daughter. True enough I dare say, but not always an easy situation.

'All right Mum.'

'Anyway, why do you have to go to London? You're there two and three times some months.'

'Phil likes to visit. We're doing the art galleries. They take a lot of time.'

'He didn't go with you last time. I saw him in town. I thought he hadn't noticed me, or he'd have come over to say *'hello.'*

I was taken aback. We'd been so careful, or so I thought. And he'd never mentioned anything to me. He obviously hadn't seen Mum, but she'd noticed him all right. I wondered why she hadn't said anything to me before. I wondered if he hadn't been on his own? I'd have to tell him to be more careful in future.

'He was called back to work. I came back the following day.'

'Seems strange to me.'

What do you mean?' I asked.

'Well all I'll say is that you're never going to get a baby if you keep spending so much time apart. That's not how it works, Christine.'

It's a good job Mum doesn't know the half of it. I smiled.

'Mum, do you want help or not?'

'You look worn out,' Marc said when he picked me up at the station.

'A lot of problems at home, and my dad's ill and mum's becoming suspicious of my frequent visits to London.'

'I see.'

'You can't, not really, but thanks. Is it far to your home?'

'No. We'll be there in under an hour.'

When we arrived in Pinner, I couldn't wait to see Marc's house. I wasn't disappointed. We drove up to a large detached dormer bungalow. It was built in a lodge style, so not typically British. It was on a close of similar properties and surrounded by several large Scots pine. It looked very 1950s to me. It was lovely, but why hadn't he brought me here before? As we pulled on to the drive Marc took my hand.

'This is it', he said. 'My home. I hope you'll like it, like us.'

The car came to a halt. My brain was just being rather slow to take in what he had just said.

'Like us?' I queried.'What do you mean?' The puzzlement obviously showing on my face.

'The reason I haven't wanted to bring you here isn't for any dark reason, Mrs Blake. It's just that ... my daughter. I have a daughter and I've been bothered about how she'd react.'

'You have a daughter?'

'Yes. She's eight, her name's Milly.'

'Is she home now?'

'No. She'll be back at three. She's shopping in town with my sister.'

'I see. Is that Julie, your sister who house-sits?' I didn't see but I didn't know what else to say.

'It is. My wonderful, older sister Julie, and I'm not just saying this but it's thanks to her and her efforts in looking after both my home and my daughter that I can get away and spend some time with you, Mrs Blake. Without Julie I'd be sunk, well and truly. She was my lifeline after Linzi died. Shall we go inside?' Marc said, 'I'll show you round and show you your room. Julie's added a few bits to brighten it, and, she's put flowers in there for you, but you can take them out at night, Julie say's that it's best ...'

'I won't be with you? I'm going to be on my own?'

'Yes, it wouldn't be right, not so soon and not with Milly here. You can see why it's been preferable to meet in our London hotel now.'

I'd come to earth with a bang. 'I understand,' I said. But at that moment I really did feel like the *other woman*, although I was not, and for a brief moment I was uneasy about everything. There was nothing I could say. I'd asked for Marc to bring me to his home. And now that he'd done it, it didn't feel good. I felt as though I were an intruder.

At three o'clock prompt, aunt and niece returned from their shopping trip. Marc introduced his daughter. She came over and said, 'Pleased to meet you Christine,' and then she sat down on the floor. She had some books with her and she proceeded to read quietly to herself. She was just like her father. She had his unruly wavy hair, and eyes that drew you in. In a few years there would be boys lining up at the door. But here, now, in this moment, I felt sadness for her. How tragic for a child so young to have lost their mother. Julie, Marc's sister spoke, breaking my train of thought and the silence.

'Hello Christine, I'm Julie. We've been wanting to meet you for months. It seems Marc wanted to keep you under wraps.' She held out her arms and walked towards me and then hugged me. 'I'm pleased we've met now,' she said, and I believe that she meant it.

She was older than Marc probably by ten or more years. She was tall and slim and seemed to have Marc's home running like clock-work. She explained that she took charge whenever Marc was away. I love doing it for him. I've time on my hands and my son's at university. In a way it helps both of us. I'm not one for joining societies. I enjoy walking but that's about the limit of my group activities. And I'm definitely not going down the road of joining the Townswomen's Guild,' she added, by way of giving me a complete mini bio of her life.

Milly was still on the floor in front of the huge fireplace. There was no fire in the grate, none was needed. Occasionally, Milly looked up at me, but after the first introductions were done, she remained silent. I wondered what she was thinking about and whether she would like me. I felt a lot would depend on Milly. She could be the make or break.

That evening Marc took us all out for a meal. We went about six o'clock as we had Milly with us. The evening was, I thought, a great success. I got on well with Julie, who told me she was widowed and that her son was at university in Warwick. She was like the sister I had imagined but never had. I knew we would be firm friends, and even though Milly was quiet, I could tell that she too, was having a good time. I was sure I could make this whole thing work.

The desperate feelings I had earlier in the day left me. This was *so* right.

Marc was away for most of August on holiday with Milly. It wouldn't have been appropriate for me to go, and I was needed more and more at home now to give Mum a hand. Dad's un-explainable, un-named condition was worsening. Phil and Nick were away. I explained it as another work trip for Phil. Mum questioned the fact that I hadn't gone with him. I explained it away with a lie.

'I could have gone, Mum, but I wanted to be with you and Dad; to help out if I can. I thought you'd be pleased I was here.'

'A wife should be with her husband as much as she can. If you don't keep them company there'll always be someone else out there who will. A man can stray. You just think on that Christine, and go with your husband the next time he's away. Dad and I can manage.'

September came and went. It was a blur of helping Mum and Dad and being a constant support for Phil, whose problems with Nick were still there. He was having a wretched time, he said. I felt like saying, *tell me about it,* but that wouldn't have helped anyone. There were no meetings planned with Marc, and I was feeling desperate. It wasn't that we didn't want to meet. It was just proving impossible.

As well as Mum's concerns for Dad, she was also bothered that I wasn't yet pregnant and wondered whether I should see a doctor. She had her finger on the pulse of all her children's situations, it seemed. I came out with waffle again. I wondered how long she'd go on believing me? I told her that we'd decided to try for another few months and then see what happened and take it from there.

JANUARY 1991

A New Year!
Mum was concerning herself over my failure to produce the grandchild she'd been pinning her hopes on for the last year. What could I say? I had to make a doctor's appointment; and I promised that's what I would do as soon as the surgery opened again after the Christmas break.

It wasn't exactly a priority for me. That was very different indeed. Top of my list was meeting up with Marc again. The Christmas holidays without seeing him were difficult to bear, but at last it all came together. I felt like a schoolgirl as I set off on the Friday evening, such was my anticipation. The time apart from him was awful. I was seriously thinking about taking him up on the offer of becoming Mrs Blake. I might even tell him about it tonight.

Phil had driven me to the station, and odd for him, he wished me luck, and kissed me on the cheek before we parted. My previous elation left me and as the train pulled out of the station, I was instead left wondering about Phil. He had a look in his eyes as I left that I hadn't seen before. A pleading? I never would say anything to Marc. That moment had gone.

Marc and I stayed until the Sunday the sixth of January; Twelfth Night, Epiphany. Phil picked me up at the station as we had arranged and he was not his usual self on the way home. There was a hollow, empty look in his eyes. I didn't know what to make of it and I put it down to the time of year. Phil hated it when all the festivities were done and everything returned to dismal normality.

Phil's humour didn't improve at all. His state of depression seemed to become worse and he remained quiet and withdrawn for a couple of weeks more. I suggested he might go and see the doctor, that perhaps he could prescribe something to lift his spirits. I didn't say anything to Phil, but his mood was pretty hard to take and I too was beginning to suffer. It's difficult to live with someone day in day out when you don't know how they are going to be when they get up in the morning or when they come home in the evening. Phil, had other ideas. He brushed my advice aside and said that he'd *work his way through it.* It had helped him before when he was down. *It just always seems to do the trick*, he had said, but at the back of my mind I was worried about him, and he wasn't opening up to me. Phil never mentioned Nick and so neither did I. There seemed to be nothing more that I could do or say, and so I did and said nothing.

My period was due on the 17th of January but by the 14th I hadn't my usual achy back. I never really thought about it though, until the 17th came and went, and nothing. I determined to hold my breath, at least until the end of the month. But I was wondering if the January meeting with Marc had, at last given me what I wanted.

FEBRUARY 1991

I'm pretty sure I might be pregnant. I haven't said anything to Phil or Marc or to my parents. I decide to let the days go by to the end of the month. I knew that stress could cause all kinds of problems with hormones and so even though I had my fingers crossed I wasn't going to get too excited, yet. By the time February reached its end and nothing had happened, I went into town and bought a pregnancy test kit from the chemist, and then I hurried home to do the deed. I wasn't disappointed. It went bright blue. We have lift off!

I phoned Marc to tell him my news. It was hard to tell whether he was pleased or not. I had never broached the subject with him. I had never told him my real reasons for starting our affair, and now didn't seem to be the right time. I wanted Marc to be happy for me, for us. He didn't say much on the phone, only, *'Are you sure?'* He seems very quiet, but I'm meeting him in two weeks, I can't wait – I do love him. I am sure that I do love him. I can't stand the silence that is coming from the other end of the phone. After a few seconds I reignite the conversation with, 'What do you think? Has the news shocked you?'

His reply is to the point.'To be honest, I don't know what to say. It's just hit me and ... it's never been something we've discussed. I suppose I'm in shock. You will be coming down to stay though, like we arranged.'

'Yes, of course. You still want me to come, don't you?'

'Yes. Nothing's changed, Christa.'

'I'm glad about that then, it's just when you mentioned being in shock. I thought perhaps me having a child would, well, I was wondering if it would change things. I don't want it to.'

'Have you told your husband?'

'He's not in yet, and I wanted to phone you first, so no, he doesn't know, but I will tell him later. I'll have to.'

'I see.'

It's late when Phil arrives home. I'm in bed lying awake and waiting until I can hear his key in the door. As he climbs the stairs I go and wait by the bedroom door.

'Well, here's a surprise!' he says when he sees me standing there.

'I'm pregnant,' is all I say.

'Bloody hell, Mrs Beacham. Congratulations!' He comes over to me and puts his arms around me. *He probably is the best friend I'll ever have.*

The following day I go and visit Mum and Dad. To say they're thrilled is an understatement.

'We're looking at some time around the 26th September,' I say.

Mum starts talking matinee coats and layettes. *Oh, how she loves to knit.*

Dad looks at me and smiles then he says my name, 'Christine.' I take his hand. My once strong Dad is now so frail, but I know that he loves me.

MARCH 1991

Morning sickness has kicked in with a vengeance. I'm just so pleased that I don't have to get up and go out to work, glad I can stay at home, in bed until the worst feeling in the world wears off. I learn that by about 11 o'clock things aren't so bad and I can face a cup of coffee. My favourite cup of tea is off the menu as I haven't been able to face tea since I first thought I might be pregnant. There's something about the smell and taste of it that is stomach turning. Later on, once I've had that first drink of the day, I remain feeling quite normal until 3 o'clock, so I have time to fit in a light lunch and even go into town for an hour if I want to.

Phil is as good as his word. He waits on me hand and foot. He wasn't too keen on me travelling down to London to visit Marc, but he relents when he can see how determined I am.

'What do I tell your parents?' he says as he waves me off at the station. 'They're bound to think it odd you going off like this. We should be doing other things like, like shopping for prams and decorating a nursery.'

'Tell them I'm meeting up with Anna. They met her once, a long time ago. We were pen friends when I was at school and I stayed at her house for a few days when I was in my teens. Mum and Dad might remember her parents, they corresponded for a while.'

'And where does Anna live?'

'I don't know where she is now. I haven't heard from her in a long time, but when I knew her she was living in Alwalton. A little village close to Peterborough. I'm sure you can bluff this one for me.'

'I only hope they remember her,' he said. And then he kissed me and saw me safely seated on the train. He had reserved a seat for me, and as Phil leaves me on the train and walks back onto the platform, again I feel something pulling me. Something nudging me to stay at home with Phil, but I can't do it. I have to go. I love Marc and I am carrying his child.

Marc picks me up at the other end of my journey. He carries my bag to the car and we drive to his home. This is a total surprise to me. I thought we would be staying at our hotel, in London, but that is not what Marc wants. On the journey, I notice him keep looking at me. If I catch his eye, he smiles. I can't tell whether it's a smile of joy or a smile of having given up. I will have to wait until we get to his home in Pinner to discover what plans he has for me.

I think it must have been joy, the smile. For as soon as Marc opens the door I can see the hallway is full of flowers, not one, not two, but six vases full of lilies and roses. He takes my bag upstairs and then comes into the lounge. He's been busy in there, too. There are flowers everywhere.

‘What’s with all the flowers? Has someone had a birthday?’

‘Don’t be silly. They’re for you. You don’t realise how happy you make me Christa. I wanted to do something special, something romantic, just for you. I can’t imagine my life without you. I won’t say anything more; the fact that you’re having my child is proof enough of what I’ve wanted to hear you say for the last couple of years, but I won’t push you. Just know that I love you Christa.’ And then he took my hands and kissed me and it was the happiest I had been for a long time. Marc really did love me and I loved him. I just hadn’t got round to telling him yet. And as happy as I was, I just couldn’t bring myself to say the words.

We had a wonderful weekend together. And as with all our time together, it just went too fast. Too soon I was heading back to home and Phil.

I had to ask Phil if Marc could visit us, at home. Marc had said that he didn’t want me doing the journey to London on my own as the pregnancy advanced. I had said that I would be fine for ages yet. At the moment I hadn’t even got a bump, but he wouldn’t take ‘no’ for an answer and insisted that I speak to Phil.

Phil was fine with the idea. I think that he, too, was concerned about me going off as well, although he never said as much. So, two weeks after my visit to London, Marc turned up on our doorstep. I was thrilled to see him. I wondered how Phil and he would get along. Phil only had my word for what Marc was like, but I needn't have worried. They were fast friends from the moment they met.

I was pleased that Phil and Marc got on so well together. It made everything simpler and I knew that towards the latter stages of the pregnancy I would want Marc here, with me. This first step assured me that things would be all right.

Mum phoned unexpectedly and Phil answered. He explained we'd got a visitor, and said could we call back. Mum, however wasn't falling for that, she told Phil she wanted a word with me, urgently. I took the phone from Phil, Mum almost fell over her words so keen was she to find out who our visitor was. I said that I thought we'd told her and Dad that Phil's cousin was coming over from London to stay for a few days. 'No, you never mentioned anything to me. And I would've remembered if you had. And there's another thing. Why has this cousin just materialised now? He wasn't at your wedding. Phil only had his uncle and a cousin from Scotland come down for that.'

I'd forgotten. Mum was sharp and remembered things right down to their last detail.

'Oh, well this is Marc, he was out of the country when we married and so couldn't come, but he's back home now and living in London.'

'I see. Best bring him round to meet me and your dad, him being family. What shall we say, half an hour? I'll have the kettle on.'

Marc and Phil just laugh when I tell them we're visiting Mum and Dad. I tell them both to get the story straight in their heads and not to deviate. I let them know that, *Mum's pretty canny, and will spot a flaw at fifty paces.*

Phil introduces Marc to Mum and Dad and the afternoon is rated a success. Marc praised Mum's baking abilities. He won her over, but not one hundred per cent. I could see from her expression that there was still some doubt there about this itinerant cousin.

'I expect we'll be seeing more of you now that you're back in the country,' Mum said.

'I hope so, if these two will let me stay occasionally,' Marc replied.

'Sometimes, I dare say,' Phil said.

Marc just smiles.

APRIL 1991

I've had my ten week scan. Everything's normal and as it should be, for me and the baby. And the midwife said there was a tiny heart there pumping away. How crazy is this? My ten week old little person is doing all this growing, and that's what my baby is, a ten week old little person; even though he or she is still smaller than my little finger.

The morning sickness that has plagued me in the earlier stages of my pregnancy has subsided now, and I'm feeling much better, and what a relief it is. I never have been a good patient. At least I no longer have to arrange my days between eleven a.m. and three p.m.

I phone Marc and we arrange to meet up. I'll be driving up to Northumberland, and Marc's arranged a hotel. I decided to leave the planning to him. I'll just drive. I can't wait. I have a lot of news to tell. I don't think Phil's too keen on the idea, he's taking the expectant father thing very seriously; but driving is easy for me at the moment, and I'm going to do it. Mum can't understand why I want to go to, *'Northumberland, of all places, and on your own.'*

I placate her by telling her that it might be the last chance I have to go anywhere on my own for a little while, and I'm going to do it. She gives me a 'look' that says far more than any words would ever do. Mum is not pleased.

She thinks Phil should be more firm with me, and she tells him that I was always strong-willed as a child, but that she thought I'd have grown out of it, and particularly now, in my condition. Phil tells Mum that I'll be all right. I'm staying in a hotel we've stayed in before, that he's sorted it, and that I'm only at the end of a phone. *What would we do without mobiles?* I hadn't realised before what a convincing liar Phil can be.

I've arranged to meet Marc in the car-park down by the river. I wait in the car park until he draws up beside me. I watch as he gets out of his car and then I, too, step out into the sunshine. Marc looks at me and then he holds me; holds me so tightly that I think he might never let me go. And I am enjoying it. If I didn't have to go back to Phil, I could quite easily stay here and become Mrs Blake. He pulls away, still holding my hands and looks at my stomach.

'You're shaping up very nicely, Mrs Blake,' he says, and then laughs quietly before pulling me towards him and holding me for the longest moment ever.

After a short stroll we drive separately to the hotel and go straight up to our room and spend long hours talking baby. I have so much to ask and tell. *Where to start?* I rattle off all my questions, tell Marc how I'm feeling, and tell him that when the baby kicks he'll be the first to know. Will he want to know the sex of the baby? I can find out at my next scan.

After a short discussion he says no, he'd rather not know the sex of our baby. He says that he's always liked surprises and that he's pleased I've not stopped surprising him yet! I'm pleased. I don't want to know the sex either. I'm just glad that I'm pregnant. And so happy that Marc's the father and also pleased, so pleased that Marc really wants this baby too. I was worried before I told him about the pregnancy. He has taken all my fears away. I know he will be the perfect father, if such a thing exists. Our weekend passes far too quickly and it seems like only hours before I leave Marc and begin the journey home.

Phil is waiting for me when I pull onto the drive. He comes across to the car and takes the case from the seat beside me. He kisses me and we walk into the house together. Over coffee we talk about the baby and the plans. I tell him my thoughts and tell him that neither Marc nor I want to know the sex of the baby. Phil smiles at me.'I'll go with whatever you decide, Chrissy.' I'm not surprised by this remark from Phil. I know that he usually goes along with everything I say *'re baby'*. 'Mother knows best', is his usual stock reply to any sort of baby talk.

When I go for my twenty week scan I feel as though I am on cloud nine, possibly higher. Everything about the pregnancy has been text book. I have a scan photo of my baby. My baby looks marvellous. I can see this little person for the first time. Somehow it makes everything real. I know that it was real before; but this scan photo is the proof, if any were needed that,

I am going to be a mum. I bring a copy of the photo home from the hospital and Phil copies it for me. The sonographer has told me that *'Everything's as it should be'*, then, she adds, smiling as she speaks, *'Do you know that your baby does a wee on average every half hour?'* That, I decide is one of the downsides to the whole thing. I tell her that it's just too much information for me.

Marc and Phil are both extremely proud. Marc has shown Milly the scan photo and she's keen to have a baby brother or sister. Phil's taken the scan photo into work. He laughed when he came home from work that night,

'They've told me I'm more like an old woman than ever! What do you think of that?'

I wondered whether his workmates had ever had any suspicions about Phil or not. I couldn't imagine that it was all just idle banter. Anyway, I didn't want to rain on his parade and he was far too happy at the moment to have me spoil it for him with a picky comment. He was, as always now, the perfect gentleman; and he hadn't been seeing Nick as much lately either. I wondered if something might be going on. Something that Phil wouldn't or couldn't tell me.

Mum and Dad had to have a copy of the photo as well. It took pride of place on their mantelpiece, framed, of course. Dad didn't say much but he smiled when I held the photo for him to look at.

'We've not got long to wait for the baby, now Dad. Only until the end of September.'

SEPTEMBER 1991

Early September was hot. And didn't I know it. My growing tum felt heavy and uncomfortable. I was forever wanting to spend a penny, and getting comfy and getting to sleep at night was almost impossible. If I wasn't hot, then the baby would decide to do a marathon kicking event. I tried to get comfy on my side and couldn't, as soon as I went to lie on my back I needed the loo again. It was a vicious circle. I decided that I couldn't wait to meet my *'little person'*, and that I wanted the pregnancy to be over and at an end. And one thing I didn't want? For my baby to arrive on my wedding anniversary. That would be too unreal. A day or two either side would be fine, preferably before. Call me odd or selfish, but I just don't like shared dates, not with anyone, and that includes my expected baby.

I was one huge lump when Phil presented me with the roses that were one of our anniversary traditions. We didn't go out for dinner that evening. Phil brought in take-away. I wasn't really hungry. Phil still wanted to mark the occasion. He didn't like any kind of family special event to go unmarked. It was the way he was.

I'd got him a card and some *Thornton's Special Toffee.* I explained why, told him that Thornton's was the closest shop to the car park. He took one look at me and said he understood, before he burst out laughing. I took one look at him and it set me off. I don't know why the baby wasn't born then and there, but it would be a few more days yet. Phil gave me some pearl earrings. I knew he cared for me.

OCTOBER 1991

Oh well, not on my anniversary, but not before either, and if the baby's not here by the tenth, I'll be induced. I hope it gets a move on. I'm not that keen on hospitals and don't want to have to be in for any longer than is actually necessary. I'm becoming fed up. Mum said it could be a boy. 'They say boys are lazy,' she said. 'If it was a girl, she would be here by now.'

I wish it was over and I could just be me again. Two people in one body is becoming too much to handle. I'm also worrying about the baby weight. I've put on twenty-one pounds. The midwife says that's good, and that I won't have a lot to lose. I hope she's right. I don't think I want to be going around looking like a beached whale for much longer. It definitely isn't flattering.

OCTOBER 7th 1991

Phil's been an absolute hero as far as I'm concerned. He got me to the hospital at eleven forty-five p.m., after what seemed like days of telephone calls to the midwife and a constant monitoring of contractions. I was so pleased when they said he could take me in. I was beginning to doubt that they'd ever admit me, that I'd probably spend the rest of my life pregnant or, the worse case scenario was that the baby would be born at home, with Phil doing the midwife bit, or in the hospital car park. As it turned out, there was nothing for me to worry about, and four hours after my admission to the hospital our son, Phillip Blake Beacham was born on the eighth of October at four in the morning. He was perfect, with a bright red face and very wrinkly, but at the same time so very, beautifully, wonderfully perfect. He weighed 8lb 2oz and was 21" long.

'He'll be a rugby player, this one,' the midwife volunteered.

'Not if I can help it,' I replied.

Phil kissed me on the cheek.

'Thank you Mrs Beacham. Thank you for my son. He's a Tuesday's child, what does that mean?'

'I don't know. I can only remember my own, Thursday. I've got far to go.'

'I'll find out, your mum's bound to know.'

'Bound to,' I said.

When Phil left me, he had a permanent ear to ear grin fixed on his face. I wondered whether he'd make it home in one piece. I told him to drive carefully and go straight to bed, but please, in the morning let my mum and dad know. I was going to ring Marc from the hospital, myself.

When I phoned Marc, he sounded elated. I was sure I was the happiest woman on the ward. I had so much to be thankful for.

'What's he like, is he like me?' Marc asked.

'To be honest, it's difficult to say. He was rather red when he was born, and I'd say he was dark, but I think most babies are dark to start with. I haven't had a look at his eyes yet, but I think they say most new-borns have violet coloured eyes.'

'You're not much help Mrs Blake.'

'I'm sorry. I'm tired. If your son would decide to make an appearance at four in the morning, what can you expect?'

'Wait until he's in his teens, then you'll know what worry and late nights can do.'

'I don't want to think that far ahead, thank-you.'

'When can I come and see you? And Phillip Blake, of course. And Milly would like to come and see her baby brother.'

'It will have to wait until I'm home. I'll only be in here for a couple of days, there aren't any complications and Phillip's doing well, feeding and doing everything else he should be.'

'I'll phone your mobile in a couple of days, just to check whether you're home.'

'I'll wait for that. I'd better go now, although I would like to talk to you for longer. I feel as though none of this is real, and yet I know it is.'

'I'll call soon. Take care, you two. And give Phillip a kiss from me.'

'I will.'

When the phone call had finished I had a flash of realisation hit me. I thought of how much more complicated my life, all our lives, had just become.

When Phil came to visit in the evening, he brought Mum with him.

'Christine,' she called down the ward as soon as she spotted me. And then she was straight to my bed and peering into the crib at my bedside. 'Can I pick him up, Christine?'

'No, sorry Mum. That's a privilege only permitted to mums and dads, and then we have to wash our hands before and after.'

'I'll just touch his cheek.' Mum rubbed her forefinger up and down his tiny cheek. 'He's lovely, Christine. Phil, you must be pleased as punch.'

I squirmed slightly, but Phil took it in his stride. 'I feel ... I feel stuck for words. But I'll get used to it. It's all pretty new you know, this *Dad* thing.'

Mum laughed. 'You and Christine and Phillip have got a wonderful life in front of you now. You're a little family.'

'Thanks Mum,' Phil said, and then, 'before I forget, what is it for Tuesday's child? Chrissy and I couldn't remember.'

And Mum was as up to speed as we knew she'd be,

'Tuesday's child is full of grace,' she said.

DECEMBER 1991

Phil always loved Christmas. And he was about to love this one even more. He was milking the 'new father' bit for all it was worth, and when anyone said to him of Phillip, *'He's just like his Dad'*, and Phil smiled, it gave me the most wonderful feeling. Phil really did love this baby. I was the one suddenly stuck for words. I usually smiled and changed the conversation on to less controversial *'baby'* subjects. I was terrified of giving some detail away and letting slip the truth to an unsuspecting friend or relative. But Phil was really enjoying every minute of the 'new dad' gig and Phillip Blake Beacham was being thoroughly spoiled. Phil couldn't stop himself from buying things. Each night when he came home from work it was with a new gift for Phillip. And since Phillip's birth, Phil *had* come home. And once home he *stayed* home. We started eating together once more. There was no mention of Nick. No mention of any male friends. He was a devoted father. Mum was right; I had a wonderful future in the offing, with my husband and son.

I hadn't had a visit from Marc since Phillip had been born. I couldn't, and didn't want to travel down to London on the train with a new baby, particularly with the Christmas holidays approaching, and Marc was tied up in London. He had wanted to come down for a visit with Milly when we came home, but I put him off. I couldn't risk upsetting anything, and Mum was coming over to see us virtually every day, leaving a neighbour with Dad for an hour or two. I felt that if I was to have Marc and Milly there as well it would have been much too awkward. Of course I felt bad about it. I did want Marc to see his son but the fact was that Phillip was two months old and his father hadn't yet seen him, but what could I do?

I thought I was making up for it by making lots of very long phone calls. Marc wasn't impressed. The tone of his voice and the abrupt responses were giving him away. I knew that to a degree it was my fault. I was the one preventing him from seeing his own son. During one of these phone calls Marc told me that he wanted us, (myself and Phillip) to spend some part of the Christmas holiday with him in London. Milly still hadn't met her little brother. *'It's not as if we can come up, with your family milling around all the time.'*

I was hurt by his words. I put myself on the defensive immediately.

'It'll have to wait until February,' I told him. Phil's in London then. We can travel down together. I'll need help with all the baby things. You can't travel light when you've a young baby.'

'You can't come before then?' He had a hardness of tone in his voice that I was beginning to get used to, but I too, was adamant.

'I'm sorry Marc. It's difficult now, with the baby. I can't just pick up and leave at a moment's notice. And to visit across Christmas would seem odd ... cause all kinds of complications here ...'

'He's my son, Christa.'

FEBRUARY 1992

In February I did travel to London. Marc had been decidedly cool in the weeks since Christmas, but then I suppose, who could blame him? I wasn't being totally fair about the whole thing myself, and yes, I really did feel bad about how things had turned out. So much so that I wondered how Marc would react when he opened the door to me, but I needn't have worried. Everything was perfect. Marc *DID* love me and for the week Phillip and I were there he was the doting Dad. And from the first moment he held me again, I realised that his feelings hadn't changed. I was the one with the problem. I would just have to get over it.

Julie baby-sat for us one night so we could go out together. I took full advantage of her kindness. She said that it was something she would do happily as long as we didn't start calling her *Great Aunt Julie.* And Milly? Milly loved her baby brother. She took photos of him doing all the various things that four month old babies do, (mostly gurgling, nappy changes and bath times) on a little camera that Marc had bought for her. All these pictures would be shown to her friends at school. At the moment she said that her friends were teasing her and didn't believe what she was telling them was the truth. 'This,' she said, waving her camera, *'is my proof, they'll have to believe me now.'*

This time with her family, her new family, was what Milly had been waiting for since Phillip's birth. She was so taken up with him and I was so taken up with everything about family life, that I said the next time we visited, I would bring Phillip to the school and meet her. I could tell she wasn't too keen. She said, *'But I'm almost ten'*. I told her it wasn't that she wanted meeting from school, it was so she could show off her new brother to her friends. Milly said she'd think about it.

So, Phillip was four months old and only just meeting his blood family. I felt bad about this of course, but the option for meeting sooner just hadn't been there, had it?

On the final Friday evening before I left for home with Phillip, just before Milly went to bed, she turned and looked straight at me,

'You will marry my daddy now, won't you?'

Marc broke in, 'Honestly Christa, this isn't a set up. I had no idea what she was going to say, but what do you think?'

'I can't say anything right now. You've both taken me by surprise.'

Milly, still looking at me, smiled weakly and said, 'Goodnight'.

Phil was there at ten o'clock the following morning to collect us. He and Marc got on famously together, which I had always found quite surprising, and I was glad that it was like that. I hated any kind of unpleasantness. I could tell that Marc was reluctant to let us go, but Phil had arrived and we had to leave. Phil took Phillip out and put him in the car seat. It allowed Marc and I time to say our goodbyes. I didn't want to leave him, and I wasn't sure when we'd be able to meet up again. No arrangements had been made. I knew then, at that point, that if Phil had said, *'You stay Chrissy. I'll explain everything when I get back. I'll tell them it's over between us.'* I know that if he'd only said that, that if the decision had been made for me; then I would have stayed with Marc. I suppose I was just weak.

Milly had gone to her dance class. Julie had taken her so that Marc could be there when I left for home with Phillip. Milly had given me a card that she had made, *'Don't open it until you're on your way home',* she'd said. I promised her that I would do as she said, and then she hugged me and drove off with Julie.

I opened the card as soon as I was in the car. I think she must have had some help from Julie, but that didn't matter, she had made it for me. Milly was fond of butterflies and she had cut out a decoupage butterfly on the front of the card. It was beautiful. Inside it just read, 'I love you, Milly'.

Suddenly I felt awkward. A feeling of elation at once dampened and my mood was lowered. I always seemed to be letting someone down. And Milly really needed someone she could depend on, not someone wafting in and out of her life at will, which I felt would be all that I could do. I couldn't imagine what she must have been feeling like this morning. The whole business was confused.

All the way home in the car I could feel Phil's eyes on me. Phillip was sleeping soundly in his car seat. He was such a pleasant baby. And I knew that when he woke, in that instant of his eyes opening, there would be a smile for me. No question.

I turned and faced forward again. Phil couldn't stay silent any longer.

'Come on Chrissy. What's the matter?'

Nothing.'

Don't nothing me. Something's happened while you've been at Marc's. What is it?'

I looked at Phil. He was so handsome. Why couldn't this be my life? I looked down. I hadn't realised I was wringing my hands. I did this when I was nervous. I must be nervous now. Must be? I was. I looked up again and across at Phil.

'Marc wants us to get married. His daughter wants us all to be together as well.'

'Is that all?' Phil replied, 'I thought something terrible had happened.'

My life was in a permanent state of flux. I was trying so hard to be fair to everyone and in the event, ended up hurting those who I most cared about, and making things almost impossible for myself. I was always telling lies to those closest to me. Having a child was all that I had wanted and I had that now but with it came more and complex problems. I vowed not to give in, not to break.

My mother was wondering why there was no baptism arranged. She wouldn't let the discussion lie. 'You were six weeks when you were baptised, still, that was in Mr Wild's time. And I was churched. A woman wouldn't dare go out or visit anyone if she hadn't been churched and children come on better when they're baptised. I'd thought you'd have known that, our Christine.'

I couldn't upset my Mum by telling her that her notion was based on an old wives' tale, that would have been too awful, and I couldn't tell her the truth, either; that we weren't bothering with a baptism for Phillip. The logistics of organising that type of event would have been too awkward, would have left a lot of questions that I would be unable to answer truthfully. In short, it wasn't worth it. Mum thought I'd taken leave of my senses, and told me so in no uncertain terms. Life was not going to get any easier any time soon.

APRIL 1992

Marc was a wonderful father to Phillip and whenever we met up we played the game of Happy Families. We became rather good at it. Milly was a wonderful sister and every time I was with them all I felt *this is where I should be, nothing else matters,* but then almost immediately the thought had entered my head, I thought of home and Phil, and knew that I couldn't leave him, no matter what. I think my decision was always going to be this, right from the start. There was never a time when I did not love Phil, that must be the reason why I resisted any commitment to Marc; Marc who was my world when I was with him, Marc who soon paled into insignificance when the miles separated us, Marc, the man who I had never told the whole truth about anything. Marc, the man I continued to deceive.

Mum of course wondered at my visits to London that I was making with almost monthly regularity, and told me I should be at home more, with my husband. I laughed off her remarks and said that I liked to keep up with the family in London, Phil's family. Mum said it was funny how Phil didn't seem to want to do the same thing. She had a point.

JUNE 1996

June the twelfth was Milly's birthday. She would be thirteen. I would be going down to London with Phillip. He was almost five now, and a handful. Things weren't as good as I thought they should be. Managing a juggling act between two homes was becoming more than awkward. It was becoming almost impossible and then on top of that things between me and Marc were pretty strained. I felt I was making these visits out of duty more than anything else and I didn't like it. I was never one to be pinned down, by anyone. Marc was becoming more and more impatient. Our meetings weren't the same anymore. The love I thought we had seemed to be slipping through my fingers and there was nothing I could do to get it back.

It was different now when we met up, when Marc and I were together in those years before Phillip was born it was somehow beautiful and special, there was an anticipation of things to come, but now, even though we all loved Phillip, I felt that sometimes I was being pressured by Marc. He wanted some sort of commitment from me; if I wouldn't marry him, what about moving in with him in London?

I couldn't do it. I wouldn't do it. I had made my mind up once and for all.

I knew that I'd never once, in all the time we'd been together, told Marc that I loved him. I always held back. It was as if we weren't meant to be together. There was an invisible bond that always drew me back to Phil. I had never stopped loving Phil, I couldn't help myself. My situation was becoming impossible, wearing me down. I really felt for the pain that I must be causing Marc, but I couldn't stop it. Phil and I agreed that Marc should come and visit us whenever he could, whenever his work commitments let him. But Phil was always there and it was awkward.

Marc and I weren't a couple, Marc was the visitor, coming up from London and staying with me and Phil. Sometimes I felt that he wasn't just a guest but that he was an intrusion and I hated him for being with us, for wanting to see me, for wanting to see his son.

And Phil? Phil was the perfect father. At home, my home, where I was Phil's wife and a devoted mother to Phillip, everything seemed idyllic. And it was apart from the usual ... Phil never, ever, came near me. There were some sporadic signs of affection, but then I knew my position. On the plus side he was a perfect father to Phillip, and since his recent break up with Nick there had been no new male friends, as far as I knew.

I never asked how the Nick thing had finally finished, but I knew that it had. I had known that there was something not quite right between them for a while, that the spark between them was losing its impetus. I suppose I didn't really want to know the details, but that it was over, as far as I could see was a good thing.

Marc had told me often that I was being stupid in my unwavering support of Phil. He said that my parents would be happier if I told them the truth; that they would be glad to know they had met the father of their grandson, and that he was in love with their daughter and kept asking her to marry him. At this visit though, for Milly's birthday, I sensed some cooling. Marc was fine with Phillip but he didn't kiss me when I walked through the door. It was obvious that things had changed, perhaps on his part too. Well, whatever it was, I would find out soon enough.

Milly didn't want to be around Phillip as much as she had in the early days. I think she found a five year old little brother a bit of a pain, especially when she wanted to be acting quite grown up with all her friends. She had long ago stopped asking me when I was, 'going to marry dad'.

She was probably quite astute for a girl of such young years. I felt for her because I couldn't be her 'mum' as well. Teenage years could be tough for a girl, and I was glad that Marc's sister Julie was there for her.

My decision to have a child had created tension in so many ways. Lives had been put under constant strain and stress. Milly was so young, so vulnerable. She hadn't asked for any of this. I had only thought of myself, and of what I thought would be best for me. But I don't think I was being selfish; I just couldn't change the way things were. My actions, everything I had done, they were all taken through a need for self-preservation.

Milly's birthday was a great day for her. I made sure of that. She spent it with ten of her friends. They went to the local roller rink and then to 'Pizza Hut', after that they came back home. I'd arranged for a local manicurist to come in and pamper them. A manicure and pedicure all round. It was all very girly and giggly. Marc thanked me for what I'd done, but it was more an 'official' thank you than a 'lovers' thank you. Things had changed then, and to be honest it wasn't a great surprise.

I waited for Marc to carry on the conversation, but he didn't. I wondered when he would. I found out later in the evening. Milly had gone to her room and Phillip had been in bed for a couple of hours. It was nine-thirty p.m. I went through to the kitchen and started to make coffee for us both. After a couple of minutes Marc joined me. (I'd left him slumped in front of the TV).

'Christa, we've got to talk.'

'I know.'

'There's no easy way to say this,' he paused.

'You've met someone else?'

He looked stunned. 'Yes, and she's free to be with me.'

'What about Phillip?'

'I'll still provide for him and I still want to see him. You'll let me keep on visiting him and you'll bring Phillip here, I hope.'

'Yes. I suppose, but will she mind?'

'Jenni. Her name's Jenni. No, I don't think so, but you won't be able to stay, Christa. That's where she draws the line.'

'I see. Where am I supposed to go then, while Phillip's here?'

'Julie's. She says that you can stay there, with her.'

'So everything's arranged?'

'Guess so.'

'When did you meet Jenni?'

'About six or seven months ago.'

'Not long, then?'

'No.'

'Do you love her?'

'I don't know what love is any more. I am still in love with you, I thought you'd know that, I've told you often enough, but it seems that I can't have you or my child permanently here with me, because of some strange logic that keeps you with your husband. I've decided to settle for the next best thing, which I think is what you've done already, isn't it?'

'Yes. I suppose it is,' I replied.

I wanted to hold him, for him to hold me but he pulled away.

'It's too late Christa, I'm sorry,' he said.

And I really believe he was.

MILLENNIUM 1999 - 2000

Phillip was nine years old and the apple of my father's eye. My dad loved it when I visited with Phillip. Dad couldn't play in the garden with him, he was too ill for that, but he would read to Phillip and play cards and dominoes with him; in fact anything that didn't require excessive effort. The good thing was that Phillip didn't seem to mind this, and he seemed to enjoy his granddad's company too.

My dad's condition continued to deteriorate and my mother carried on as best she could. I continued to help her but Mum was stubbornly independent. I think sometimes that's where I get my attitude from. And yet I know that my mum wouldn't have done any of the things that I'd done, and that if she knew my story; if she knew the truth of my life, it would probably change our relationship forever. I knew it would never change the way she felt about Phillip, and that was good, because I felt that Phillip was the one honest thing in my life and I couldn't even think of how my life would have been without him. What I'm trying to say is that, *Phillip was my life.*

Mum didn't want Dad to go into a home or into hospital, unless it had to be that way, or as a last resort. She wanted to look after Dad at home, and my help was, I think, sometimes too much. I sensed that sometimes I was too overbearing. I tried to organise too much, I was an intrusion, but I couldn't let Mum do everything on her own. I had to try and be diplomatic quite often. Not easy for me. I had to try and strike a happy balance, one that satisfied both parties. At times it was difficult to achieve. Mum and I were so alike, there was bound to be friction from time to time. And there was. Mum reminded me often that it was, *'her house'*; that was when I knew I had gone too far and it was time for me to take a step back and for a silence to be observed.

My father was virtually housebound and could only get out of the house with the help of two people who had to support him, one on either side. The longest journey he had made in the last two years was from house to garden seat; and that was a tremendous effort for him. He took perhaps six steps at the most and each one was extremely difficult. It was a terrible ordeal to see a man reduced to this, particularly a man like my father who had been so strong and active. As a child I had thought him a super-hero, there was nothing he couldn't do. Now I was left to see him like this, the husk of the man who had once been there. Mum though, was determined to look after him at home for as long as she possibly could. She didn't want outside help or assistance. That would mean she was admitting defeat, and she couldn't do that. She wouldn't do that, because she loved Dad, and that love meant the two of them being together.

I honestly don't know how my mother coped with everything, I wondered if I could look after Phil if I found myself in the same position. I decided it was a question I couldn't answer. But maybe you don't answer these questions until they're asked; until an answer is demanded of you.

We didn't do much celebrating for the millennium. It wouldn't have seemed right, not with all the turmoil in the family. Phillip had saved some of his pocket money and bought a blow up champagne bottle and Phil and I let him stay up to see the fireworks on TV. That was as celebratory as we got. My father had just died; December 31st 1999, at six o'clock in the evening.

My father's death, when it came, happened peacefully at home. It happened where and how he and Mum would have wanted. They were both together in the home they had shared all through their married life. Mum phoned me to let me know. She'd already spoken to my brothers. They were both at the house when Phil and I arrived. Phillip was with us, but we didn't let him see his granddad. I asked Mum why she hadn't phoned me earlier. Had she noticed a decline in Dad's health, I wondered?

'We wanted it to happen this way,' she said, 'just us two together.'

I had no right to argue with it, but I wished I could have said, '*Goodbye*' to my dad.

So that was our start to the millennium, and it meant there were more pressing things on our 'to do' list than parties and celebrations. Dad's funeral had to be arranged.

On Monday, January 8th the family filed silently in to St Alban's church. It was the church where my parents had married in 1948. Mum didn't cry.

Easter was in April, late April. The 23rd was Easter Sunday. Arrangements were made for me to go down with Phillip and see Marcus. Well, it was really for Phillip to see Marcus, to see his dad. Marcus didn't exactly spoil Phillip, but he went very close to it. I just let it run. What could I do? I'd lost all my rights as far as telling Marcus what to do when I'd refused to leave Phil and marry him. I always felt that Marcus was in some way punishing me for my decision.

I stayed with Julie at her home. We always had a good time when we met up, we were really very good friends.

Marc and Jenni took Phillip on days out and as always seemed to be the case they let him eat burgers, too many than I thought was good for him, but I couldn't reprimand Marc and Jenni over this, after all Marc was his father, and Phillip had to spend some time with him. There were also lots of chocolate eggs to be had. So many in fact, that a number had to come home with us, to join the others that we had left there. Phillip had enough chocolate to stock a small shop.

Marcus and Jenni had been married now for three years. They had no plans for children, not yet. Jenni was a career woman and still only twenty-nine years old. Julie told me all this. It made me feel quite old but I was still only thirty-seven myself, just about. I would be thirty-eight later on in the year, in August. August was the time when I had arranged next to go down to London with Phillip so he could meet up with Marcus. Marc would visit us in June, just for a weekend. Whenever he came up to visit he was alone. I don't know whether Jenni was trying to avoid us, or she couldn't spare the time off work. Marc always seemed to be telling us how busy she was. It seemed to me that they were nearly as far apart in their married life as Marc and I had become. The only difference being that I wasn't married to Marc.

My birthday was the 26th August, Saturday. I was travelling down with Phillip on the Monday before, the 21st. Phil said that he would celebrate with me on my return but I knew that he would've made sure that Phillip had something to give me for 'the day'. Whether I would see Phillip on my birthday remained to be seen. That I suppose would depend on Jenni, and whether Marcus had remembered my birthday. I hadn't had a card from him since he married Jenni and it upset me. What harm would a birthday or Christmas card have done? I felt useless and forgotten. I just hoped and prayed that he would never forget Phillip so easily. Would Jenni be able to call time on that relationship as well?

When I came down on the morning of my birthday Julie was already having breakfast in the kitchen. A pot of tea was brewed.

'You look all in and you've only just got up,' she said.

'It's my birthday – thirty-eight today.'

'Happy Birthday. I'm sorry, I didn't know. Marc should have reminded me, he knows I'm not good with dates, but let's not dwell on that now. We should do something special. Let's go somewhere for lunch, my treat, and I won't take no for an answer.'

'We won't get in anywhere at such short notice. And it is Saturday, it could be very busy.'

'Don't you worry about a thing. I'll sort it out. We're going out, ok?'

'Ok.'

The weather was quite warm but it was showery and there was a light wind. It wasn't blue skies and sunshine. Not the weather you order in for birthdays. Nothing was how I'd planned or imagined it would be. I know Julie was trying to cheer me up. It was obvious there was to be no card or gift from Marcus or Milly. If there had been Julie would've passed them on to me. It was as though I had become invisible. I didn't think they could've forgotten me so easily. I had considered that my previous birthdays hadn't been forgotten, maybe just lost in transit; the fault of the post office or some other carrier. Birthdays were something that I made a point of never forgetting.

Perhaps I was just being silly. Marc had nothing to do with me anymore. The only reason I was here was because he was Phillip's father. I should remember that, and also remember that he was married to Jenni. Jenni was his wife. I had made my choices; I had got what I wanted, hadn't I? And Milly? Milly was seventeen now, a young woman. Why should she remember me? I was maudlin, I knew that. At least someone had remembered me, my mum. I went to my bag and took the card from its envelope. The front read, 'To a dear daughter', then inside just the two words, 'From Mum', and a kiss.

Mum wasn't happy about this visit but she didn't say anything. I think she was just hoping my 'lone trips' would eventually become something that was in the past, something to be forgotten, and with Marc married and me staying with Julie, well perhaps her thinking was that there was less for her to be worried about.

By lunchtime the weather hadn't much improved but Julie insisted we were going out.

'Where?' I queried, knowing that she'd be lucky to get anywhere at such short notice.

She tapped the side of her nose. 'You'll find out when we get there. It's a surprise.'

Julie drove to the centre of town. She'd managed to book a table for we two at the 'Queen's Head' in Pinner. When we walked through the door the place was packed.

'What strings have you pulled to get us in here?'

'It's who you know, sometimes Christa. Jason works here, he's on the bar. I phoned and made the reservation. I think they've managed to squeeze a table in at the back for us.'

As we walked to the bar to be seated, Jason spotted us.

'Hi Mum. Just follow me.'

I noticed that Jason was tall with a shock of black curly hair.

'And you must be Christa,' he said, looking at me.

'Yes that's right.'

'I remember you visiting Uncle Marc years ago. I don't suppose you remember me?'

I felt awful. I didn't remember this young man at all.

'I'm sorry, no.' I replied.

'Don't make Christa feel awkward, it's her birthday,' Julie said.

'Happy birthday,' he replied, with a cheeky grin.

He then seated us at our table and went to bring the menu.

'Just come to the bar to place your order when you're ready.'

'No special treatment then, not even for your own mother?'

'No, sorry,' he answered and went back to the bar smiling.

I thought it odd that Jason would be working in a pub after studying and getting a degree. Julie must've seen the cogs turning.

'You're wondering why he's here, aren't you, and not at some hospital or abroad saving the lives of undernourished and misplaced children.'

'I wouldn't be as blunt as that Julie, but the last I heard he was studying medicine at Warwick, and now ... this.'

'It all seems a long time ago now. He's been working here three or four years – and he likes it. Couldn't seem to hack it in the work place after university. He didn't seem to fit in anywhere but then a friend had some summer work here, they needed extra staff and he mentioned it to Jason. He's been here ever since. And, who knows, in time he may go back to medicine, but for now, this is the day job.'

'I wasn't prying.'

'I know. Come on, let's look at these,' Julie waved a menu in front of me as she spoke, 'And decide what we're eating. We've got to celebrate.'

It all went well after that. The food was excellent and I surprised myself by ordering a strawberry cheesecake for dessert. It was while we were having our coffee that I spoke my thoughts out loud.

'I wonder where Phillip is today, what he's doing? I thought he might've phoned with it being my birthday. I feel as though I've been forgotten.'

'No Christa. I don't think that at all. Phillip's bound to be thinking of you. You're his mum. He'll probably phone you tonight. Marcus and Jenni have probably taken him out for the day.'

'Does Jenni like him? I worry about that when he stays. I worry that she might upset him or be nasty to him in some way, because of who he is, because ...'

'Jenni loves Jenni. I won't say anything else on that, but Marc wouldn't let anyone or anything hurt Phillip.'

'Thanks for telling me that, and thanks for all this as well. It's been lovely.'

I raised my wine glass in a toast. My birthday wasn't going to be so bad after all.

*

When Phillip was born we'd decided, the three of us, Marcus, Phil and me, that Phillip should call Phil 'daddy'. After all, Phil would be the one bringing him up. He would be the one who was there when he fell over, the one watching him play football and cheering him on. He would be the one attending parents' evenings. He was the one named as father on Phillip's birth certificate. Even so it was a tough decision to make, but the three of us made it with the best of intentions. Yes, I did want Phillip to know who his father was, I really did; and I did believe that he must always know that Marc was his real father, but I also knew that he would have to call Phil *daddy* for the sake of everyone involved. For the sake of family, for the sake of *my* family. This arrangement would also give Phil and I a sense of security knowing that no one need ever ask or suspect. It had to be done and it was what we agreed.

I had hoped that Marc would always be fine with this arrangement; but I suppose it's easy when you're the one always with a child. I suppose you can easily fall into believing that once a decision's made that it will never need to change, but life's clever at putting obstacles in front of you, of forcing you to make different choices. So, I should have known it would eventually become more difficult for the parent left isolated; and that parent was Marc. It seemed the longer things went on as they were, the more impatient Marc became. He said he was beginning to feel like an outsider in his son's life. He didn't like the fact that Phillip called him 'Marc'. I didn't know what to do. This was a new problem that I hadn't foreseen.

Phil broached the subject with Marc and put it to him that if he wasn't happy with the way things were he should come up and visit while we sorted things out. It would be easier for him to come to us than for the three of us to make the journey down to Pinner.

Phil also suggested that we could perhaps go ten-pin bowling as Phillip liked that and it would be somewhere we could chat, neutral territory as it were. Marc agreed. He came up a couple of weeks later. I was glad to see he arrived on his own. I didn't want Jenni to say anything that was remotely connected to the upbringing of my son. She hadn't any children. How could she know or contribute anything?

Phillip enjoyed the afternoon, and we adults, I think we put off right until the last minute any discussion that we were supposed to be having. It was difficult, but we explained everything to Phillip as we went along. Phillip didn't really seem remotely interested in any of the things that to us seemed enormous obstacles to be overcome. He asked a few questions and then just said *'Ok'*. That was it. Problem solved.

We should have realised that nothing as momentous as this is ever so straightforward. It was later, on the way home that Phillip asked, 'So who is my real daddy?' I had to relay the story one more time; tell Phillip that Marc was his father, that without Marc he wouldn't be here. That Marc was special because he let Mummy have a baby.

'And my dad, he is still my dad?'

'Yes, he is,' I replied.

I told Phillip that no one else need be told, and that it was our secret. As far as we were concerned at home, we were just Mum and Dad, but that Marc ... well that he could call Marc *dad* when he visited him in London. We explained to him that it was his special secret; that it made him special and no one else was to know, not even Grandma.

We assumed it was all sorted out now and that this time Phillip really did understand. Phil and I also assumed things would be easy for us now, uncomplicated.

With hindsight, I guess we were behaving more like children than Phillip, the one we were trying to protect.

Back in 1991, I really believed that eventually I'd be with Marc; that I would marry him and that we'd be the happy family I'd always dreamed of. I also hoped that Phillip would understand how everyone loved him and that he was special to us all.

Thinking of what we'd done, or should I confess now and say because of what I'd done, what I'd done in my desire to become a mother; I should've seen that there'd be problems. And Marc, Marc didn't even know the full truth of the affair, I still hadn't told him all these years later, and now that he was married to Jenni, what was the point of giving him a history lesson? None at all, I decided.

The only person who knew the complete story was Phil. That I had my son meant everything to me and for that I was thankful every breathing moment. I just didn't think of the problems there could be along the way. I suppose the answer was that I didn't want there to be problems, and so I put them to the back of my mind, out of the way. But they were always there, weren't they, waiting for me.

One problem was Milly. She shouldn't have been but she was, albeit through no fault of her own. Milly was Phillip's half-sister but when Phillip came home from a visit to Marc and said that he hoped *'Milly was his real sister'*, Phil and I just carried on living in fantasy land. It was a case of, if you put your head in the sand for long enough and ignore things, eventually they will go away. This state of 'ignorance is bliss' didn't last. I had to drag my head from the sand and do some more explaining. It was Phillip who started the conversation, a conversation I had hoped would never happen.

'If Milly's my sister, why is her daddy my Marc?'

It seemed to me as though all the explaining in the world always seemed to leave another question, particularly from an inquisitive child. I felt agitated, angry. I tried to explain without losing my temper, but it was difficult. I ploughed on,

'I've told you, we've told you. Marc is your real daddy, but you have to live here with Mum and Dad who live here. It's just how it is. And Marc, you can call him 'dad' when you stay with him and that's ok too, you know that'

Phillip looked at me as I explained everything over again, as if taking it in for the umpteenth time but I felt trapped, as though I was in a kind of limbo, not really knowing whether there was any more I could say that would make it easier for a boy of nine to understand. I felt frustrated, awkward, inadequate, and I was tired of explaining. I felt as though I was tying myself up in ever tighter knots. The more I said the more confused Phillip became. I left the conversation hanging, the questions unresolved.

I decided that I would put my faith in Phil; Phil, who was usually brilliant in sorting things out. My faith didn't help me much this time, though. I told Phil what Phillip had said, how the conversation had centred around Milly but Phil wasn't much help in the matter. In the end I just asked him point blank what he thought we ought to do, his reply wasn't helpful.

'I'm his dad aren't I? I'm the one bringing him up, doing all the important stuff. I'm his dad. That's all he needs to know.'

I was annoyed. This was a side-step from Phil and one that I hadn't expected. 'But you can't just say that, we've told him about Marc. Marc came here. It was your idea to have him visit and sort things out, once and for all. We all agreed, or have you forgotten about that? I thought Phillip understood but he obviously didn't and now it's becoming a worry. I don't want Phillip to be upset but I don't know what to say, and I definitely don't want him saying anything to Mum. She wouldn't understand. And who could blame her?'

'He won't be upset. I'll have a word with him later.' And with that last comment Phil got up and left the room.

I knew I daren't phone Marc as there was always a chance that Jenni might answer the phone and I didn't particularly want to have her pass messages on to Marc, and besides Jenni seemed to revel in causing problems for me. If Jenni answered she could be awkward, would be awkward, no question about that. It was like walking a tightrope whenever I rang and asked if Marc was free to speak, either to me or to Phillip. I sensed that she didn't like the contact I had with Marc. She didn't like the connection I had to him. To put it bluntly, she didn't like me.

In the old days, before he was married to Jenni I would've phoned Marc at work or on his mobile. I couldn't do that anymore. Marc had put a stop to it in the days before he was married, and he'd changed his mobile number. I suspected that Jenni had put her foot down. I tried to argue that I might want to contact him urgently, if there was a problem with Phillip, or an accident. He said it would be fine for me to *'phone his home number'*.

Nothing was going right. I'd made a bloody mess of everything. Everything apart from Phillip was a sham. My marriage, my life; the lies I had to tell my mother. And all this to keep my one perfect secret safe. All this to keep Phillip safe.

*

I thought that Mum was coping quite well after the loss of Dad. I'm not saying that she didn't miss him or think about him and grieve, but she was very independent and seemed to bounce back into her old life and routine. Me? There wasn't a day I didn't think of Dad. I was his daughter and I had to grieve too. I hadn't lost anyone this close to me, not as an adult, and it was awful. Some days it seemed as if everything was back as it should be, and the next I was back on the downward spiral. I wished it would pass. I didn't want to keep feeling this way.

In mid September Marc phoned me. He said that he wanted to have Phillip visit next half term, in October. He would come and pick Phillip up, that he wanted Phillip to stay with him and Jenni for the holiday. I told him that I had planned a trip to Devon for Mum and that it was only for a few days but that Phillip was coming with us, that there was no way he could go down to Pinner again, we'd only just arrived home.

Marc wouldn't take no for an answer. He was as adamant and as dictatorial as I had ever known him. He said that he would come up and collect Phillip himself, that Phillip would be all right and that Jenni would be there with him in the day. I felt uneasy, but Marc was Phillip's father. I had been squashed into a corner.

OCTOBER 2000

The day of Marc's visit arrived. I hadn't yet told Mum that Phillip would not be coming to Devon with us. Phil kept saying to me, 'the sooner the better', but I refused to take his advice and before I knew it we were in October, and then we were here and I was on the other end of a telephone and speaking to Mum, trying to explain myself and my actions. As soon as Mum heard my words, 'Phillip wouldn't be able to come with us to Devon,' and once she had recovered her disappointment she was adamant; adamant that she wasn't coming with us to Devon either. The only reason she had agreed she was coming was because Phillip would be there. The whole thing had turned into a complete shambles. Marc was due to arrive to collect Phillip in half an hour. It was now ten o'clock. At ten-thirty, Marc duly arrived, prompt as always, and he and Phillip were ready for the off. I was on the phone to Mum as Marc popped in the door. Mum wasn't budging. No amount of talking would make her change her mind. If Phillip wasn't coming to Devon, then neither was she. It was chaos.

'But you can't do this, Mum,' I argued, 'Phillip's going now, Marc's here and we'll be round to pick you up in about fifteen minutes.'

'I've told you Christine, I'm not coming, and that's that. You and Phil go off and enjoy yourselves, but it'll be without me.'

'Mum, I'll phone you back. I'll have to go now and see Phillip and Marc off, don't go anywhere, stay where you are, ok? All right, speak to you soon. Bye.'

'Awkward moment?' Marc asked.

'Just a bit. I told you we were taking Mum to Devon for a few days but she's now decided she doesn't want to come. It's because Phillip won't be there. But you knew what our plans were when you phoned, didn't you? And yet you still came down heavy-handed and laying down the law. I'll speak to her later, try and talk her round.'

'I'm sorry. I didn't want to cause problems for you. I just wanted to have some time with my son.'

'But you've had time. Phillip was with you in August, or can't you remember?'

'I think we'd better go. Is Phillip ready?'
We all came out of the house to wave goodbye to Phillip and Marc. It seems awful to think of it but even though I was angry with Marc and the way he was treating us, I was willing Phillip and Marc to be off so that I could go inside and finish off the conversation that I'd begun with my Mother.

'You'll be a good boy for Marc, now.' I said. Phillip smiled at me as he slid into the back of the car. 'Of course, I always am,' he replied.

'Of course he will be,' Marc said, and he smiled at me. Then in a moment, he came over to me and hugged me.

'I still love you, Mrs Blake.'

I looked round to see where Phil was, he wasn't there. For a second, it was as it had been all those years ago. And I knew that whatever had happened between us, and whatever paths our lives had taken, whether we were meant to be together or not, that part of me still loved this man. Whether I had ever loved him enough, I don't know, probably not. But Marc's words shook my world, left me in a daze, like they had when I had first met him, in the hotel, all those years ago. I struggled to compose myself.

'Take care of him for me,' I said, and then added, 'and Phillip, look after your Dad.'

Marc smiled at me again and got in the driver's seat.

'Are you all fastened in there, Phillip?'

'Yes, Marc.'

'Well I think we're off 'hen.'

'No.' Phillip said. 'Where's Dad? He always waves. Where is he?'

I looked round. I thought Phil would have followed me out. He still hadn't appeared.

'Hang on, I'll go and see where he is.' I hurried inside.

'Phil, Phil, where are you?'

'Here, in the hall. The phone went as I was coming outside. Your Mum's had a fall. She's been taken to A and E.'

'Is she all right?'

'As far as I know. Let's go and see Phillip off and then we'll get down there. We won't mention Mum's accident, best not to upset him.'

And that was how we left it. Phillip and Marc drove off and Phil and I hurried to the hospital.

'You've taken your time getting here,' Mum said, as we both entered the ward where she'd been taken.

'All right,' I said, 'What's happened?'

'I've had a fall.'

'I know that. Where were you?'

'In Mr Hudson's, the greengrocer's. He phoned for the ambulance.'

'I told you to stay where you were, that I was going to phone you after Phillip and Marc had left. Why did you go out Mum?

'It was only to the corner shop, to Mr Hudson's. I knew it would only take a minute.'

'But what did you need that couldn't wait? I told you I was on my way.'

'Folk can change their mind you know, Christine. You also told me that Phillip would be coming to Devon with us. You went and changed your mind about that one, upsetting me. And all because Phil's cousin shows up from London, you'd only just been down there to see him. I don't understand all this lot. It seems a funny way of going on if you ask me. I thought you'd have put your foot down, Phil. You seem to let that cousin of yours walk all over you.'

'Look, it doesn't matter, any of this. Let's just get you sorted out Mum. We can worry about Devon later. Ok?' Phil said.
Mum smiled. I looked at them both, Mum and Phil. I could tell it was bothering Phil, but I had to keep some face in front of Mum.

'Well?' Phil said, and looked at me.

'Yes, I suppose. Let's sort you out, Mum.' I said.

I looked at Mum. She suddenly looked smaller to me, older; and in that moment, that instant, I couldn't blame her for anything. And she'd no idea what Phil and I were up against. She was just being Mum and saying what she felt.

'It was good of Mr Hudson to get the ambulance, Mum. The nurse has just told me that they want to keep you in overnight for observation. They're satisfied you've not broken anything. This could've been serious, Mum. This could've meant surgery. Lots of people your age break bones when they fall. You've been very lucky.'

'Yes. They told me I was strong. I said to them, I've always eaten well and I like liver and onions. They laughed. But I know I'm right.'

'You are Mum. I'll stay with you now for an hour, until visiting's over. Phil can go home and sort things out there. Then we'll both come back to visit this evening. They've told me to phone in the morning after ten o' clock. If you're Ok we can come and collect you.'

Phil kissed Mum on the cheek and told her to be good and he'd see her later. He squeezed my hand as he left. There was no kiss for me, but that wasn't unusual.

'Where's Phillip? I thought you'd have brought him with you.'

'You know where he is, Mum. He's gone to stay with Marc for a week. If you hadn't changed your mind we'd all have been going on a holiday. You'd have been coming to Devon with us, although the way things have turned out, it's perhaps as well we're not going.'

'Don't try and make what you're doing sound right, Christine. Phillip spends far too much time with Marcus. He's only Phil's cousin. Why should Phillip need to keep going down there to London, or away with Marc at holiday times? It's not right Christine. It's not right at all.'

Our Devon trip was cancelled and we lost the cost of the accommodation, but that was small fry in comparison to all that was going on; and if I thought this was hard work I didn't know what would be handed to me a few days later when Phillip returned with Marc.

It was about eleven o'clock in the morning when the phone rang. I answered it. It was Marc. He said that he was bringing Phillip home, they'd had to cut the visit short. Would it be all right? They would arrive at about three o'clock.

'Is there a problem. He's not ill or anything?'

'No. Nothing like that. It's ... Well, I'll speak to you when we get there. It might be best if Phil's there as well.'

'What's happened? Is Phillip ok? You're worrying me now, Marc.'

'Don't worry. He's fine Christa. It's just that Jenni's been her usual helpful self and taken it upon herself to tell Phillip his life history.'

'I don't understand. Phillip knows everything, what can she have said that Phillip didn't already know?'

'I can't go into all the details, but it's the way Jenni says things. She can make the most innocent remark seem like it's going to end in the death penalty.'

'What?'

'You heard. But we'll talk later. I have tried to calm Phillip, but he just doesn't want to stay here any longer. Jenni's ruined it for the both of us, and I know she took great pleasure in doing it. In the meantime, do you want a quick word with Phillip before we set off?'

'Yes please.'

It reassured me to hear Phillip's voice but I couldn't wait to see him. I could tell he was upset. What did Jenni want from us? I was pretty certain that she didn't like me, but to take her anger out on a boy; well it was just too much. Roll on three o'clock.

When Marc and Phillip arrived, Phil and I were waiting. Phillip immediately ran to Phil and hugged him. Phil hugged him back.

'Come on, tiger. I'm glad you're back. Had a good time?'

'You are my dad, aren't you?'

'Of course,' Phil replied.

'Good. I'm glad. Can I go upstairs and play for a while?'

'Course you can. I'll be in to see you in a little while. If you fancy doing a roadway with your Lego, I'll help. I just need to chat to Marc first.'

'Ok.'

Phillip looked brighter now he'd been reassured by Phil. We three went through to the lounge, and then I made coffee.

'What's Jenni said?' I asked.

'She's told Phillip everything, no holds barred. I don't think she went as far as to say that you and Phil didn't love him, nothing like that but she's said that I'm his real dad, and that he should really be with us. She's got him so totally confused that he won't listen to anything I say. We'd always got on so well, but he ... he just wanted to come home, to his mum and dad.'

'Our son was not up for discussion. He knows you're his dad, we've told him, thank goodness. Was Milly home?'

'Yes. She's furious. She told Jenni that it was none of her business and she should've kept things to herself. They're neither of them speaking now.'

'Good for her,' I said.

Phil was more practical. 'What exactly did Jenni say?'

'She's told him I'm his dad, but it's not strictly what she said that's the problem. It's more about how we met, Christa, she couldn't wait to spill everything.'

'But to a child? And anyway, our meeting and what went on between us has nothing at all to do with Jenni, but you Marc, did you discuss us with Jenni?'

He looked first to me and then to Phil.

'I know it was wrong, I knew I shouldn't have said anything to her and as soon as I'd spoken I wished I could take the words back.

'You discussed us with Jenni?'

'I'm sure you mentioned us to Phil, so don't suddenly come all innocent, but it would have been better all round if I'd kept quiet, but I didn't and now, well believe me, I would've stopped her if I'd known what she was going to do but I'm afraid by the time I heard about it from Milly, the damage had already been done.'

'Why should she do that? It seems to me she just wanted to make out that I was some sort of scarlet woman. That everything between us was cheap. Well it wasn't like that at all.'

'Christa, I'm sorry, believe me I truly am sorry. We'd had a row. It was to spite me.'

'I suppose I had to come into it somewhere, then,' I said.

'I'm afraid so. Whenever we argue, which is often these days, you always seem to feature Christa,' Marc said, then added, 'but that's not the point at the moment. We need to talk to Phillip. We need to put him straight. We can't risk any gossip or tittle-tattle coming from anywhere else. I suppose we're all to blame. And now ... now everything's coming back to bite us, and our foolishness.'

Phil went and brought Phillip downstairs. We stumbled and tripped over our words, Marc and I, but then Phil took over and he made everything sound so wonderful that I could hardly believe it for the truth myself, but it was. It also made me remember that for a short time I had truly loved Phillip's father. Marc and I let Phil carry on.

Afterwards, Phillip just wanted reassurance from us all that his life wouldn't have to change in any way from the life he knew here, with us.

Of course it wouldn't. I wouldn't let it. I smiled at my son but I was wondering how often we'd have to go through this. I didn't know how much more I would be able to take.

'So you are my real dad,' Phillip said to Marc.

'I am, and I'm proud to be your dad. And you must never forget Phillip, we all love you and care for you and each other, and that's what matters most in life.'

I could hardly believe what I was hearing after all the fuss Marc had caused.

'Is Milly still my real sister?'Phillip asked.

'She's your half sister. She had a different mum. But Milly's real mum died. But she is most definitely your sister.'

'And I can still live here, with mum and dad?'

'You can,' Marc replied.

'And do I have to visit you and Jenni again?'

'Do you want to?'

'Not if Jenni's there.'

'That's fine. I'll sort something out and we can just spend time together, the two of us. We'll have boys' time out, you and me.'

'Ok,' and then Phillip held his hand out to Marc, 'Let's shake on it,' he said.

After that we all felt as though a weight had been lifted from our shoulders, even though it was the same conversation we had had many times before. I hoped this time that Phillip finally understood and thought that perhaps before we were all expecting too much from him.

Marc left to go back to Pinner.

NOVEMBER 2000

One problem solved, another one waiting. Phil and I still had Mum to consider. Things hadn't gone quite so smoothly there as we'd expected them to. They'd kept her in hospital for another two weeks. It was a strain on us all. Mum wanting to be home, but the hospital saying that at the moment she wasn't well enough to be at home. There didn't seem to be anything making her ill. There was nothing you could say was causing her to be there. She just wasn't picking up.

We told her we'd bring Phillip to visit. We told Phillip just to, 'Chat to grandma, there's no need to mention anything about his visit to Marc and Jenni.' That side of our family problems we felt were best kept to ourselves.

'They won't let me come home', Mum said, as soon as we were at her bedside.

'No. The sister's just said they're moving you to a convalescent home for two weeks. And then you can come home, all right?'

'If you say so', she replied.

'I've got a card for you Grandma, open it,' Phillip said as he approached his Grandma's bedside. Mum put her hands on Phillip's cheeks and squeezed him. He made as if he was embarrassed, but I could tell he was glad that his grandma was still ready to make a fuss of him.

'Oh, I'm all the better for you coming to see me,' she said as she took the card from him. She opened it, and read what Phillip had written, 'Get well soon Grandma, we want you back at our house'.

'That's marvellous, Phillip. And look at all the kisses! How could I fail not to get better?' And smiling she placed it with the other cards on her locker.

After Phillip's visit, Mum seemed to rally a little, and the following weekend was deemed fit enough to be moved to a convalescent home. The hospital had made all the arrangements.

There was a communal lounge, very nicely decorated. A lot of 'G Plan' type furniture and patio doors that opened out onto a lovely garden area. Being late autumn, there wasn't that much to see in the garden but it was such a lovely space, and Mum's room had a view of the garden as well, but she wasn't pleased, not at first viewing.

'The lounge is lovely', I said, trying to sound upbeat. Mum wasn't in an agreeable mood 'It'll do', she said.

I smiled. I felt as though I had had the life slowly drawn from my body. As a last ditch attempt to salvage something from the situation I offered,

'I bet they play cards in the evening after supper. You've not been able to play since Dad died, well here there must be someone who would play.'

'I shouldn't think so Christine. They'll all be on their last legs. That's what these places are for.'

'Mum, come on. It's only for a fortnight, and they've a hairdresser. You can have your hair done. That'll be a treat for you.'

Mum perked up at that. That was one thing she'd missed then, not having her hair done!

The next Friday Mum had booked herself in to see the hairdresser for a shampoo and set. She was being 'done' when I arrived in the afternoon to visit. I waited silently watching as 'Mr Jason' cut and snipped and set. Mum kept calling him 'Mr Jackson', but he didn't seem to mind. It looked nice when he'd brushed it out and given it a spray of some lacquer. I told her so.

'No', she said in earshot of Mr Jason.'No, I don't reckon much to his cutting. He's no technique.'

Nevertheless, she took the compliments about her hair and sang his praises to the other residents. I guess that's just 'Mum', and there was nothing would change her now, not at her age. We'd better just keep on smiling and go with the flow!

The next time I visited Mum I thought how well she looked. I kept my thoughts to myself, but it was reassuring. She was particularly pleased when I told her that the 'two Phils' would be calling in to see her on Saturday, after Phillip's football practice. She smiled, and then continued to remind me,

'You're lucky to have a husband like Phil. Many a one would only wish to be so lucky. Just remember that,' and she looked at me and smiled again.

I sat and just looked at her for a moment. Mum was quite shrewd. I wondered if she had ever guessed at my situation, or if she had known all along what was actually going on. And I did think on what she'd said, and whatever the situation, I knew that my parents had both been genuinely fond of Phil, loved him as a son, in fact. And then I told myself something I'd always known. I was actually in love with Phil, I couldn't deny that. There was some bond between us that could never be broken. And Phil loved me and he was good to me, and he loved our son. He did. We were a happy family. Why should I still have doubts?

I took Mum's hand, squeezed it gently and then kissed her on the cheek.

'Right, I'll say goodnight now and I'll try and get in again before weekend, but remember, my men are visiting on Saturday.'

'The two Phils,' she said.

'Yes, that's right.'

At home on the Saturday, I was alone. Phil had taken Phillip to football practice and they wouldn't be home until mid-afternoon, after they had visited Mum. I felt I was on auto-pilot. I was performing household tasks and getting them done but all the time my mind was on Mum. I knew things weren't right with her. She looked well enough, but there wasn't any light in her eyes, there wasn't any spark left. She looked as though she were ready to give up. Phil had told me not to worry. He said that he was sure that when he visited with Phillip he'd find things ok.

'She was probably tired, that's all.'

He put his arm round me offering reassurance, I suppose. It did little to quell my fears. And then he surprised me.

'Chrissy, I love you.'

I looked at him, 'I know,' I answered.

My feelings, my worries about Mum were rubbing off on Phillip as well. I didn't mean them to but it just happened. Phillip was a sensitive child and perhaps I should have tried harder not to let any feelings show. I suppose I was tired and let my guard down for a minute on one too many occasions, but that's all it takes, one unguarded moment; and children know more than they ever tell us. They can keep a lot bottled up inside if they think that it's better that way. I know now that Phillip did. It was while we were in the kitchen, before he left with Phil for football practice. Phillip was sitting at the kitchen table, watching me as I cleared away the breakfast things. I could feel his eyes almost burning through me. I knew he wanted to say something but I just carried on with the job in hand, hoping the moment would pass. It didn't. Eventually Phillip suddenly asked, 'Is Grandma going to die?'

'No, of course not. Why do you ask?'

'You've been sad lately. Your face has lost the happy look. I wondered if Grandma wouldn't come home again. And ... you look like you did before, when Granddad ...'

He was interrupted by Phil calling from the hall.

'Come on, the team'll be waiting.'

'I'm coming,' Phillip said as he scuttered out the door, mouthing a quick goodbye to me as he left.

I was glad the conversation had been drawn to a halt. But I knew Phillip was right. I was wondering whether Mum would come home again.

DECEMBER 2000

Phillip's birthday had been and gone; October and November passed and here we were making plans for another Christmas. Phil, was as usual busy putting his plans into action. The light display was in situ outside, now it was the turn of the inside of the house. I left him to it, Christmas was his favourite time of the year. The time when the big kid in him took over. And he was perfect at keeping Phillip occupied. I was still worried about Mum and I couldn't seem to concentrate on anything. Phil kept everything moving smoothly along.

My brothers, Ken and Bill said they'd feel happier once Mum was home. I knew what they meant. She was still in the convalescent home. We were all hoping she would be home with us for Christmas, but it seemed a long shot. During the period of convalescence she'd had two more stays in hospital. She was re-admitted once for two weeks, then again for ten days. Each one was only a minor blip, but I wished so much that she'd pick up and be able to come home with us. I suppose age does catch up with us all eventually and Mum wasn't getting any younger. She'd missed Phillip's birthday party. That upset both of them. Phillip had not known a birthday or a party without his Grandma. I suppose it was a milestone of growing up, of finding out that things very rarely stay the same as we would want them to.

If Mum was ok, I would hear by the 15th December, Friday. The home had said that they would phone and let me know as soon as they could, after the doctor had finished his weekly round. The decision to discharge was entirely up to him. The call could be any time between eleven a.m. and twelve noon.

The 15th was also the day that Phillip finished for the school holidays. I'd said that if she was well enough and could come home that Mum should come to us first and stay for a week or two. It would gently get her into the swing of things again. She would be able to think about going back to her own house after the holidays. Surprisingly, Mum also thought it a good idea.

With this in mind, Phil had decorated the spare room for her. It was a bit of a copy cat of her bedroom at home. We thought it might help her to settle. The walls were very pink, and Phil had papered over the headboard wall in a lovely pink, silk relief paper. We knew that Mum would like it.

It also meant that for the first time in ages Phil and I would be back in our own room, together. Even though Nick was long gone and there had been no further lovers for Phil, as far as I knew; Phil and I had kept to our own rooms. I wondered how we would cope, but Phil was my husband after all and since Marc had married Jenni, I too was without a lover. It would seem strange, that was for certain. But

Phil, ever the gentleman had taken account of everything. He wouldn't share the bed with me, not tonight. He came into the bedroom complete with a sleeping bag, pillows and blankets. I had nothing to worry about; at least that's what Phil said. Me? I knew it was right for us to be back together like this. I didn't want to have nothing to worry about.

DECEMBER 15th 2000

At ten o'clock the convalescent home phoned me. Mum was deemed well enough to join us for Christmas. The home had already been informed of the plans we had put in place and they were more than satisfied that they were adequate. If we had any problems at all we were to call them, we were not to feel isolated. They were at the end of the phone and we weren't to forget it.

Phillip was pleased when he arrived home from school to see his Grandma sitting in 'her' chair in the lounge. She was equally thrilled to see Phillip. Ken and Bill called round and said that Sheila and Carol would come in and sit with Mum if I wanted an hour or two to myself. Mum was pleased to see them. They hadn't visited her much while she was in hospital or at the convalescent home, but she was pleased to see them nonetheless.

Mum asked, 'Are all the family coming here for Christmas, as usual, Phil?'

'Wouldn't be Christmas without them,' Phil replied.

I was just hoping and praying that everything would come together. I had another small problem to contend with, a problem no one else knew about. Marc had started to call me. He wanted us to start meeting up again, regularly. I said I'd think about it, and let him know once the holiday was over.

It made the time approaching Christmas more worrying for me than ever. I felt that he was putting me in a position that I didn't want to be in, that I was unsure about and it meant I spent a lot of the holiday wondering what on earth was going on in my life. I thought Marc and I were through, after all he had a new wife; I had resigned myself to that. I was also resigned to the fact that any contact between us would now be purely on a friendly basis, when we had anything to discuss regarding Phillip. I thought of us as an amicably divorced couple, but then when he called me, when I heard his voice on the other end of the phone, well then I wondered what it was I really wanted? I wished someone could tell me what I should do. I truly was split between Phil and Marc. I knew that it shouldn't be that way, not at all but I just didn't know what I wanted anymore. I felt as though my life wasn't my own. I was living it entirely for other people. I was trying to be whatever others wanted me to be, and that was difficult. I felt trapped.

All this uncertainty made the Christmas day celebrations stressful. I don't know whether I hid it well or not, but I felt as though the day was a viewing day, and I was the one being viewed. I felt as though I was giving all and sundry the opportunity to say, *'Look what she's done now, she thinks we don't know, but we do. Everything about her is a fraud, a fake, but we'll string her along anyway. See how far we get before she snaps.'* It definitely took its toll on me as one minute I was fine, and enjoying myself with my family, and the next minute I was wondering what to do about Marc, Phil, Phillip and Mum. It was one of the most difficult times I had ever had to live through; and the trouble was that at the bottom of it, I knew that the problems I had were all of my own making. I had only myself to blame for the way things had turned out. Even so, I did try to put Marc at the back of my mind and I tried for the sake of my family to throw myself into the festivities. Phil enjoyed this time of year so much and I didn't want to put a dampener on anyone's enjoyment, after all Phil and I were the hosts. And Phillip, none of this was his fault and he was just so happy to have Grandma home. I had to try and keep up the pretence, and so that's what I did. In the end, I think I must have pulled it off quite convincingly as everyone said what a good time they'd had, and Mum, who was lauding it a bit now she was back from the home and hospital, had a great time holding court and showing off her newly decorated bedroom. She must've climbed the stairs more in that one day than she had for the previous seven.

'I'm glad she likes it,' Phil said, 'anything to keep her happy, eh?'

'You don't mind her being here, do you?'

'No. Your Mum's always been great to get on with. If it was up to me, she could stay forever. I like having her around, and although she does have her awkward moments, she's generally good company.'

'She thinks the world of you. And she still tells me how lucky I am to have you.'

'We get on ok me and you, don't we?'

'We do.'

'Partners.'

'A great team.'

They were my final words on the subject and the conversation ended. I'd liked it to have gone on a little longer, probed a little deeper but Mum returned with her entourage. Another group of friends to do the tour, another group of friends who would no doubt be suitably impressed by the lengths Phil had gone to, to make his mother in law comfortable. I was surprised by the sheer number of Mum's friends who had decided to drop by on Christmas day. Mum of course wasn't.

'I've always lived hereabouts. I've known most of my friends since school. We always think of one another, why shouldn't they pop in?

'No reason', I replied. 'No reason at all.'

Phillip had, for the first time done his own Christmas shopping. He'd bought some lovely chocolates for Grandma. He knew that she had a chocoholic's sweet tooth. I received some lovely fingerless gloves that I'd admired a few weeks earlier. My admiration of them had obviously stuck with Phillip. Phil received a Christmas tie that was no sooner unwrapped than it was on. He laughed and gave Phillip a hug. Phillip beamed from ear to ear. He loved it when things went right.

He'd bought Marc a box of hankies with his initial 'M' on them. We wrapped them together and then I posted them. I couldn't say anything; I didn't want to upset Phillip but I felt that handkerchiefs, even monogrammed ones, weren't quite the right gift to send to your dad; it wasn't enough, somehow. I know that my own father had received hankies year in year out from me when I was small, but I couldn't equate that with now, and Phillip. I was tying myself up trying to figure it all out in my head, so that I would be happy with it. It did no good. Part of me felt, or should I say wanted, the gift that Marc received from Phillip to be special; to be father and son special. I wondered whether hankies did that, then another part of me was thinking, well they're from Phillip, Marc will be thrilled. Phillip's saved up his pocket money and made the choices. Marc will be delighted. Then I wondered if the real problem was with me. Was it that I was just going over and over continually in my mind, the choices I'd made when I'd fallen for Marc? Was it that I couldn't come to terms with those choices and I was placing the burden of this on my son's shoulders?

Phil was his usual Christmassy self and proudly sporting his tie form Phillip. It had Rudolph the red-nosed reindeer on it, and when you pressed the nose, the tie played a selection of Christmas songs, and yes, you've guessed, number one was *Rudolph the Red-Nosed Reindeer.* Marc hadn't really featured much this year for Phillip. There were still the visits to

London, but they were short, three or four day affairs, and for reasons best known to Jenni, Phillip didn't spend any of the Christmas holiday with his dad; but Marc hadn't forgotten Phillip. In fact he'd gone overboard with the amount he had spent on gifts for his son, so much so that I'd actually taken the step of phoning him, hoping all the while that it would be his voice I heard and not Jenni's when the phone was picked up. I asked him what he thought he was doing being so extravagant, but Marc was his usual charming self, and explained everything away. So much so that I ended up being the one feeling bad. And when I was feeling at my lowest that was when Marc struck the killer blow. He wanted to know why it was that I had curbed the visits this year? I stumbled over my words, 'No, I haven't done anything, Marc. It's just the way things happened, and ...' and then I stopped. I was ending up explaining myself, giving excuses for things that I hadn't done. *Just a minute,* the thoughts raced through my head, *didn't Marc want to start meeting again, wasn't it only weeks ago he was phoning you continually, day after day.* Marc's voice broke the silence and he proceeded to give me reason after reason why he'd had little access to his son. *I was jealous that he was happy with another woman, I had to have Phillip close to me so that I could 'turn him' against his real father, I wanted him to 'hate' Jenni.* My resolve ended. I gave up. It was no good trying to explain or tell Marc any different. When he was in this frame of mind there was very little any one could do. He would believe what he wanted to believe. I decided it best to leave the conversation there. I wished Marc and Jenni all the best for Christmas and the New Year. There was no response from Marc; the phone was just put down. I heard the click as the receiver was returned to the cradle. I was in the middle again. I couldn't understand Marc, he changed like the weather. A few months ago he held me and told me that he still loved me, and I believed him, even though I knew it was wrong to have feelings for this man who was married now to another woman, and I loved Phil, didn't I? I always had. The love I'd had for Marc had never been strong enough for me to want to commit to him; this man who was the father of my child. I felt wretched. All I seemed to be good at was hurting people.

It was a day or two later that Marc phoned me. I was expecting him to carry on where the conversation had left off previously, but it didn't. He was the Marc of old and he rather took me by surprise.

'I've never stopped loving you, Christa. I know now that I always will love you. Is there even the remotest chance that we could marry? It's ... my marriage to Jenni is ... is almost at its end. Neither of us is at fault, not really, we've more or less agreed that we married the wrong people. We both want different things.'

'I don't know what to say Marc. This is a shock to me.'

'We both know though, don't we, I mean it's obvious to anyone that we're meant to be together?'

'I need time to think about this, I can't say anything, not now. I'll call you up in the New Year, we'll talk.'

New Year's Eve was quiet but we didn't mind. I don't know why I'd never thought of it before, but I suddenly got to wondering what Ken, Bill, Carol and Sheila did for the New Year. Whatever it was, we were certainly never invited.

Mum was sitting in the chair by the TV, waiting for Big Ben to chime, sweet sherry in hand.

'What do Ken and Bill do at New Year? I asked.

'Same as this, I suppose,' she replied.

'What, they stay in? Altogether or at their own homes?'

'I don't know. Together, I should imagine.'

'They never ask me and Phil.'

'No. Well they're close, brothers usually are.'

'That's it?'

'Yes.'

'And you never go, then, or did you go when Dad was alive?'

'Oh no, we were never asked.'

'I see'.

Phil came in from the garden.

'Where's Phillip? John's out next door. He's setting up some fireworks in the garden. Do you want to go and watch? It'll only be for a few minutes.'

Phillip had wanted to stay up, but the pressure of trying to keep his eyes open had become too much for him and he had fallen asleep on a bean bag in the corner of the room.

'Nudge him, gently,' I said, 'see if he wakes up; if he doesn't, leave him and we'll go out and watch.'

Mum's face lit up. 'Can I bring my sherry?'

Glasses primed, we paraded through to the garden, they'd already started the counting down ... seven, six, five, four, three, two, one, 'Happy New Year!'

There were flashes and fireworks and singing and ... Phil kissed me, as a husband should kiss his wife, and then he whispered in my ear,

'I love you, Mrs Beacham.' And he held me close. I felt like jelly inside. I was actually quivering. Then he was light hearted again, he held my hand and then grabbed Mum's and said, 'Come on,' and we went and joined our neighbours, who were busy forming a circle in the garden.'*Auld Lang Syne'* was done to death.

As we walked back inside our own house, we could see Phillip was on the bean-bag. He was still asleep.

JANUARY 2001

I knew this was going to be an eventful year. I knew that some bridges would be burnt and that others needed rebuilding. I was determined to get everything in my life sorted out, once and for all. Whether I'd be able to keep a clear head and steer myself through, I didn't know, but I was sure as anything going to give it a try.

Marc phoned me on the 5th January, a Friday morning.

'When will you be coming down?'

'What, just me?'

'Just you. I need to talk. I need to talk to you, about us.'

Before Christmas Marc had said that he wanted us to be together and I'd fobbed him off again, and then a few days later he'd phoned and angrily asked me why I was restricting his access to Phil and when I'd remonstrated with him he'd hung up on me. That hanging up of the phone had made me see red. I *would* not make contact with Marc. I would leave everything to him now. I would not be bullied by Marc and Jenni; but now that he'd phoned me I felt that he'd put me on the spot. I faltered and paused for a while as the thoughts went racing though my mind, then I blurted out the words.

'There can't be any us. I thought you'd realised that; and it'll look a bit odd, won't it, me coming off to see you on my own? And Mum's living with us at present, so it's difficult.'

'Could you at least try, Christa?'

I tried to stay calm and focus on what needed to be said. I did not want this to end up with us shouting at each other down the phone.

'It's not like it used to be Marc. You're with Jenni, now. You're married. And I can't meet you on my own. It's not right, not anymore, and Phillip ... he can't come, he's back in school.'

'It never used to be difficult for you to get time away ...'

'Well, Phillip was younger then. And, you weren't married, and now, Jenni ... well I know that she doesn't take kindly to Phillip being around, and I know what you told me a few weeks ago, that your marriage is pretty much over, but it isn't over, is it? We can't do this to ourselves Marc, we've both got to try and look to whatever the future holds, but it can't be a future together. It's not going to happen. And Phillip's just had the Christmas holidays, you know that. I can't let him take time off school. It wouldn't be fair. He'll fall behind, and not only that, the staff don't like it either. Out of term time you more or less have to jump through hoops before a child's allowed to take a day off.'

'I didn't know it would be so difficult.'

'Well it is.'

'I need to talk to you.'

‘We’re talking now.’

‘Don’t be sarcastic Christa. I know that remark isn’t really you talking. You’re not like that.’

‘I don’t know what I’m like anymore. I have trouble just convincing myself that I’m me.’

‘Have you and Phil got problems?’

‘No. The only problems I have are my own.’

‘I see. And I suppose that has something to do with me?’

‘No, you don’t see, and I can’t blame everything on you, either, but I can’t explain. It’s too involved.’

‘When can you meet me? I could come down to Northumberland. We could go to our hotel.’

‘You’re going for the hard sell, Marc. We don’t have any ‘our hotel’. This has got to stop.’

‘Come on. I’m not that bad.’

My resolve faltered. ‘Look, I’ll see what I can do, but it’ll have to wait a week or two. Mum’s here with us now, but she might’ve gone back home by then. If she has it’ll make things easier for me. I’ll perhaps be able to stay over a weekend. I’ll see what I can do. I’ll phone you soon. I promise’

‘No Christa. I’ll phone you. I’ll phone a week tomorrow, the 13th. You might have something worked out by then.’

‘I’ll see what I can do. Leave it with me.’

I went up to Mum’s room. She was reading.

'You've been on the phone a long time. Who was it? '

'Marc. Phil's cousin.'

'Oh, him. He's a funny one, he is. I'm not keen on him. He's different to Phil, they're nothing alike. Still, I suppose they're only cousins.'

'Yes,' I replied, 'only cousins.'

I told Phil about Marc phoning. I thought it better that he heard it from me than from Mum, and I didn't want him to feel that I was keeping anything from him.

'What did he want?'

'He'd like to see me, in a couple of weeks. What do you think?'

'I'd rather you drifted apart from him. It will be best for us all. I know we all agreed on a number of things when Phillip was born, but things have changed. You are my wife Chrissy, and on top of that I don't think it's good for Phillip, particularly now he's getting older. And look at all the fuss we had last year after Jenni put in her six penn'orth of handy advice. I know I can't stop you going but ... I think things should cool. Let things take their natural course, eventually that's what has to happen. We can't all be tied to each other forever.'

'You really mean that, don't you?'

'Yes, I do. I think it's time we thought about us, about our family. We shouldn't risk it Chrissy. We're pretty good together. And we're totally different people than the ones we were when Phillip was born.'

'We are?'

'Yes, of course we are. I don't just mean us, either. I mean all of us. That includes Marc and Jenni. Marc's remarried and made a life for himself. We should do the same. I don't want you going off with him again, Chrissy. It isn't right, and it isn't good for you, either.'

Mum came through to the kitchen.

'Don't stop on my account,' she said, 'I've only come through for a glass of water.'

I laughed, 'We're about done. I was just telling Phil that Marc had invited us down for the weekend.'

'Mmph. Too much of it,' she grumbled, and went back into the lounge with her drink.

Mum and Phil are pretty much on the same wavelength, I thought. Phil said, 'We'll carry on the conversation later, upstairs. We'll be able to think more clearly.'

'Ok.'

I smiled at Phil, but it was another of those times when I felt as though my inside was doing somersaults. I just wanted everything to be ok. Why couldn't we all seem to get on anymore without someone or other putting the other party under pressure? Maybe I was wrong all those years ago when I thought it would always be as perfect as it was the day Phillip was born. Perhaps I was always the eternal optimist.

Mum had gone to bed by nine, closely followed by Phillip. Phil and I had thought that we might struggle to get some time to ourselves to talk, and knowing tomorrow wasn't a school day, we thought Phillip might have played for time as he often did when the weekend came around. Not so tonight. We were in luck.

I went and made coffee for myself and Phil. It was more out of a sense of, *'This is what we do'*, not because either of us really wanted a drink.

Phil and I then sat in a kind of shared artificial silence; neither of us speaking in case it induced conversation from the other one. And in any case, we'd agreed that later was the time for the real conversation. We drank the coffee slowly. I think we were both putting off the inevitable. Dragging the time out. I had the feeling that neither of us really wanted to discuss things.

Upstairs, I sat on the bed, waiting for Phil to come back from the bathroom. He came through and plonked himself next to me. Knowing that eventually someone had to break the ice, I spoke.

'Well,' I said, 'where are we?'

'I don't want you to go and see Marc. There's really no need.'

'I don't think I can just cut him out of my life like that. He is Phillip's father, after all.'

'Well treat him like who he is, like Phillip's father. We've always let him see Phillip. We've never denied him that. And, as I said earlier Chrissy, he's married now to Jenni. He has a wife. They should be together. They should be left to get on with their lives.'

'But they're unhappy. You know what he said.'

'Precisely, what he said. We haven't heard Jenni's side of the story, have we?'

'But Phil, what about what she said to Phillip? We know what Jenni said to him, Phillip told us. Surely we should believe our own son?'

'Yes. But what had driven her to it? We don't know what they were arguing about or why she said what she said but they're married Chrissy. It's up to them to sort out their troubles. We need to stay well clear of it.'

'You think so?'

'I know so. And from what you told me of the telephone conversation, it's you he asked to go and visit. Did he mention Phillip at all?'

'Not initially, but he knows that I've always taken Phillip with me. I've never visited without him, not since he's been born, and you know that too, Phil. But I did tell Marc that it would be almost impossible to get the school to allow him time off, particularly as they've only just returned from the Christmas holiday.'

'I'm just reminding you that it's you who he wanted to visit him, no one else, not at first. You want to be aware of that, and also be aware of the fact that he's married now. When you first met him he wasn't, and that made all the difference. You don't want to be involved in the break-up of his marriage, if that's what it comes to.'

'I don't think it would come to that. Marc's already told us that he and Jenni don't get on; it's nothing to do with me. And he is Phillip's father. He has some call on me.'

'No he doesn't have any call on you, Chrissy. He's married, we're married. The only connection between us is Phillip. That's where everything should begin and end.'

'Mum would agree with you, but there's something else. Marc told me that he still loves me.'

Phil turned to face me, where I lay on the bed. He put his arms around me and kissed me. He kissed me as he had a few days earlier, on New Year's Eve.

'I've told you I love you Chrissy, and you're my wife. It's me you're married to, not Marc.'

'I know, but your friends, the ones you had when we first married, and Nick? That was going on for a long time, and I know you've told me there's nothing going on now, and you're home most nights and you're good to me and Mum, and I know in my heart of hearts that Phillip could never have a better father than you, that no one could have cared for him like you have; but the doubts are always there with me. I find myself asking, *When will my world here fall apart?* I suppose what I'm really asking you is how can I believe you? How can I be sure?'

'How can anyone ever be sure of anything? There hasn't been anyone since Nick. And now with Phillip, our son, I have realised that it's really been you all the time, Chrissy. It's you I've wanted, needed, all the time. It's always been you Chrissy. I just didn't know it. And if you need me to say any more, all I'm going to say is, *I love you.*'

'Phil?'

And then the light was turned off and Phil kissed me again and I kissed him back and for the first time in our marriage I made love with my husband.

And I knew then and there that this was for real. This is where I should be. It had taken Phil and me a long time to get to this point, but the fact that we'd arrived was more than worth waiting for.

The following Tuesday, the 9th January, Phillip was back at school. It gave Mum and me some time to discuss arrangements. Would she be returning home?

'I don't know. I've liked being here. It's good having company.'

'We won't push you out. Phil has said that you can stay on here as long as you like. We'll have to go and check your house though and make sure it's secure. Do you want to come across with me? We could go now, and after we've done that we could nip into town, have a look at the sales. What do you think?'

'I could do with a new coat.'

'Come on then.'

Number ten, Etherow Walk was still standing.

'Garden looks ok, considering,' Mum said.

We went inside; everything was just as it had been left when Mum was taken into hospital. The only difference was that the house felt lonely, un-lived in. It didn't feel like Mum's house anymore. It wasn't the home I'd grown up in.

'We'll pop over again in a few days,' I said.

'I mightn't come with you.'

'That's all right.' I said, and we got in the car and headed for town.

The shops were busy, very busy. The sales had drawn everyone out. A lot of people were buying things just because they were reduced. They'd probably realise when they arrived home with their new purchases that they didn't really need them at all.

Mum must've been in half a dozen shops and tried on every coat in her size before she finally settled on one she liked. She'd always been a fan of Donegal tweed. It seemed it was quite popular again.

Phil was back in work at Radford's electrical contractors. He didn't spend as much time away as he had done early on in our marriage. In fact I think he was sometimes under my feet more than I would've liked. But our home life was bliss. Marc hadn't phoned in over a week, so I assumed that everything had cooled, and maybe he was on better terms with Jenni; and Mum seemed settled with us. In fact it was more than that, everything about the move seemed right and I would go as far as to say that Mum was virtually back to her old self. Bill and Ken called in to see her occasionally and I know that she got a lot out of their visits, even if they didn't stay for very long, but as far as Carol and Sheila were concerned, well, they had rarely ventured over the door step since Mum left the convalescent home. I think they were worried they might have been asked to do something, but there was nothing for them to do, and Mum was fine with me.

FEBRUARY 2001

February 17th, would be Mum's birthday, and we were planning a surprise for her. We'd booked a table for four, (just Mum, the two Phil's and me) at the 'Grey Goose'. It was a small, family run pub with a restaurant. The daughter of the previous landlord had now taken over the reins and she ran it with the help of her husband and their two daughters. It had a small dining room at the back and there was just enough room to fit six tables in, anymore and it would have been squashed. It was where Mum and Dad used to go when they had something, anything, to celebrate.

This birthday would be Mum's eightieth. Phillip had helped to choose the cake with me. (Although I did have to steer him away from Sonic the Hedgehog). We finally settled on a plain sponge cake, iced with Mum's favourite flower, anemones.

The legend was simple, 'Happy Birthday, Mum.' I knew better than to have asked for candles or a number signifying Mum's age. It wouldn't have gone down well at all.

The distance between my brothers and me was widening. I didn't really understand why, and after Christmas, Phil had said that there'd be no more big family parties. He just didn't want it. I could go along if there were invitations coming our way, but he didn't want to be a part of any more big occasions.

Phil said that from now on it was going to be just *'Us and friends'*. I said that he'd always put on a big show at Christmas, that he'd always enjoyed the big family do. He just replied that he wasn't going to provide Christmas for everybody, he couldn't do it. *'What about us?'* I'd asked. *'We'll all still enjoy it,'* he'd replied.

This made me think. What had happened for him to say this? Had my brothers or their wives or anyone said or done something that had offended him? Phil didn't take offence easily. It just wasn't in his nature but there must have been something said or done, I was sure of it; but whatever had happened, Phil wasn't confiding in me. I decided to leave things as they were and not do any deeper digging. I was always of the opinion, least said, soonest mended. I also knew that we were the ones who usually did the inviting, the organising of family events. I couldn't see any random invitations coming our way.

There was no point in asking Ken or Bill anything. They never gave anything away. Even as children they stuck together limpet like, and would refuse to talk for days if the mood so took them.

And that was the end of it. Whatever Phil was doing he must have had good reason, and so I left it there. There was no point in carrying on a conversation that wouldn't have achieved anything. I had to support my husband. The gulf between me and my family had just widened further and there seemed to be nothing I could do to stop it. My only real concern was Mum; what would she say? She was bound to have a point of view and she wouldn't be afraid to voice her opinions. And family was family, whatever the problems, family must come first, that was what Mum was bound to say. I knew it.

Mum was sitting in the lounge, gazing out of the window when I walked in.

'Are the boys coming?' Mum asked me.

'What do you mean?' I said, hoping that I'd hidden the surprise in my voice at her asking so awkward a question.

'To the pub for my birthday.'

'How did you find out about it? It was supposed to be a secret.'

'You can't live in a house with someone and have secrets, even if you think you can,' she said.'I know everything that's going on.'

'Then you'll know that we're all going, the four of us.'

'I meant my boys, your brothers, will they be there?'

'I don't think so, we've not heard from them, have you?'

'No, nothing. No one's phoned or anything. I think they've forgotten me.'

I put my arms around Mum and hugged her.

'No Mum, they'll be in touch soon. They'll have planned something special, you'll see.'

'No. I doubt that.'

'They will, or Carol and Sheila will. They won't let this special one go by, you'll see.'

Mum smiled.

'It's not right for family to split apart, not when they don't know why there's a split. And that's what you're doing. If your Dad were here, he'd ...'

'Don't say things like that, Mum. You'll get upset and well ... Dad wouldn't like that.'

I made some tea and sat with Mum a while longer. We were both quiet, neither of us daring to give anything away. I was wondering what Mum made of it all, these arrangements that had been made for her birthday, but instead of saying anything, instead of voicing my feelings I just kept looking at her and smiling. I didn't really want to talk anymore.

As Mum's birthday approached, she became more and more agitated. There was still no word from Ken and Bill.

'Phone them for me, Christine.'

'What would I say?'

'I don't know, just chat to them. You're their sister.'

'Well you can do that Mum, they're your sons.'

'I don't like.'

'I'm not thrilled by the idea, but if you want I'll dial and when it's answered I'll put you on. If it goes to ansaphone you can leave a message.'

'I won't do it now. Maybe tomorrow.'

She didn't phone the next day or the day after that, and neither did I, but when it was the fifteenth, two days before her birthday, I heard her on the phone.

'Ken, it's Mum. Are you ok? I'm fine. I just wanted to invite you for my party on the seventeenth. It's at the Grey Goose. You're all invited. Be there for seven o'clock.'

And then she just chatted on for about another ten minutes before coming into the lounge. She didn't notice me at first.

'What have you done, Mum?'

'Invited my sons to my birthday party, that's what.'

'Have you spoken to Bill as well then?'

'I did that earlier, while you were in the bathroom. They can all come.'

'When you say all, do you mean the children as well?'

'Yes.'

'But Mum, there mightn't be room. Phil only booked for the four of us, now it's going to be twelve. You just can't do that. You should have mentioned it first.'

'I'm fed up of waiting for you. I thought I'd better take things into my own hands,'

'You should've said what you were going to do. We'll have to phone the pub now to book more seats, if we can.'

'Well of course you can. Have you ever seen it really full in there?'

I had to admit that I hadn't.

Phil wasn't too pleased by the arrangements that had been made by Mum, but he understood how I'd been more or less backed into a corner, even with everything that she'd done, Phil thought a lot of Mum. She would be forgiven. She was watching TV when Phil walked into the lounge,

'All right Mum?'

She smiled, 'Yes, fine. Has Christine told you there's been a change to the plans for my birthday?'

'She has Mum, but it's ok. We thought we'd go out just our immediate family, but if you want everyone there, that's fine.'

And it was. Mum's birthday was lovely. She loved her family and to see her happy was what it was all about, wasn't it?

When the bill needed to be paid, Phil got up and went to the bar; my brothers had already left the table, kissing Mum before they did so. Neither of them came to me or went across to the bar where Phil was left to settle the bill. I suppose there could have been a misunderstanding, Mum did invite them after all, but no one thought to ask, to offer. Carol and Sheila were herding their respective children together and getting ready to leave. They went and hugged Mum and thanked her for inviting them. They waved to Phil and mouthed a silent 'thanks' as they left the pub. I went across to Phil, who was still standing at the bar.

'Shall I go after them?'

'Best left, Chrissy. You go back to your Mum and Phillip. I'll sort it out, there's no point in having any upset.'

It seemed some things never change. This was the pattern as it had always been. I'd just never thought about it before. I don't think I'd taken much notice of anything, but Phil had. And it must have eventually come to a head. He'd didn't want to carry on paying for the rest of my family to enjoy themselves. And why should he?

'We got over that one all right anyway. And I know Mum enjoyed herself.' I said to Phil later. He didn't answer me, he just nodded, which I took to mean, *'Leave it there,'* and I did.

In the morning there were other things on my mind. Easter wasn't far away. I would have to contact Julie, get some plans in place if Phillip was going to spend some time with Marc. It wasn't something I was looking forward to; it was just something that had to be done.

'Something that had to be done'. That was how my life was feeling at present. It was as if I was being confronted by a huge check-list where each item had to be ticked. Miss an item and you were in trouble. The problem was it was a never ending list. I felt that for every one thing I ticked off and felt good about, pretty soon it would be replaced by two more things. The harder I worked, the longer the list seemed to become.

Marc was either on the phone and impatient and wanting to see me or Phillip, and angry with me if nothing could be arranged or a week would go by with nothing at all.

It was during one of the angry calls that he'd mentioned that he might apply for custody of Phillip. I wondered whether it was a way to undermine me, this almost prescribed ultimatum. A way to make me go along with what he wanted or these are to be the consequences. Phil said that Marc would be bluffing, that it wouldn't come to that but I wasn't so sure.

Marc had said that he wanted time with Phillip at Easter and I had agreed. I would have to steel myself and sort it out. I really felt as though it was all beginning to seem rather forced, and each visit Phillip made to Pinner to be with his father filled me with more and more resentment.

Marc was always a kind and loving father to Phillip, but the reality was that I was beginning to wonder whether all this to-ing and fro-ing was worth it.

Mum had remarked on my quietness over the last few weeks. I just said that her birthday had worn me out. She wasn't taken in, '*You didn't have to do anything,*' she said,' *we all went out for a meal!*'

I let the next week go by but by the Wednesday of the following week I couldn't put it off any longer. I rang Julie. I needed to know what was happening. Marc too, was being very quiet and that always made me feel uneasy. He was the one who'd brought up an Easter visit. Why had everything gone so quiet again? There were a lot of things that I felt needed an explanation.

'Hello, 678951.'

'Julie, it's me.'

'Oh.'

'Yes, can we talk now ... is it ok?'

'If that's what you want.'

'What I want?'

'Yes.'

'Julie, I want to know what's going on. I'm worried to death here. Marc hasn't phoned and you didn't get back to me, about Easter. Is everything all right?'

'All right?' What do you think?'

'I'm sorry, I don't know what you mean.'

'That's terrific, coming from you.'

'I beg your pardon. What am I supposed to have done'

'You tricked my brother into giving you a child.'

'Just a minute Julie, it's not like that. It wasn't like that.'

'I know what I know. Marc's told me everything.'

'He has?'

'He wanted to marry you, I know that. I know he wanted to give his son a home. A son deserves to be with his father.'

'I'm Phillip's mother Julie. I come into the piece somewhere you know. He's my son.'

'Marc's his father.'

'But my husband's brought him up. Phil's always been there as his dad. That was what we decided, Marc and I, it was what we decided.'

'And Phil, you're surely not telling me he played no part in this sordid little affair of Happy Families?'

'Julie, I don't like your tone, but I'll ignore it, that's not what's being discussed, and

I'm sure if you asked Marc he'd tell you the same thing that I'm trying to tell you now if you'd only listen and that is, that we all decided. The three of us and yes, Phil was part of the discussion because it was fair and right for him to be included. Phil's my husband; he was going to be bringing up another man's child for goodness sake! So, the three of us, we decided that right from the start we would be straight and honest with our son; not only that, we came back to it over and again when Phillip was younger. We had to, because we had to be sure that Phillip knew that Marc was his father. His biological father. It was decided upon because we knew that what we were doing was for the best. We had our son to protect. And Phillip was always uppermost in our mind, always. Phillip knows that Marc's his real dad. He's always known, from being little. Can't you see that? We've always been honest about it, all of us, but then I suppose we have to thank Jenni for stirring up a hornet's nest with her unfortunate loose talk to a nine year old. I'd have thought you'd have agreed with me, with us, on that at least, Julie. And I might just add that Jenni made all of her contribution without a word to Marc.'

'Marc would have totally backed Jenni up, she's his wife. That's what couples do.'

'So are you telling me Julie, that everything the three of us discussed and decided, the three of us who are directly involved with Phillip's welfare, that it has no bearing now on anything and we should leave things to Jenni, the miracle worker.?'

'There's no need for sarcasm Christa, and I'm not going to take sides on this.'

'It seems like you already have.'

'Marc is my brother, and Phillip is my nephew, and I can tell you now that Marc never thought like that. He wanted to have more of a say in his son's welfare, but Marc being Marc, well, he let you have your own way, as usual. I told him after we'd spoken about it that he'd been much too soft with you, but that's Marc. You see, he thought you'd also agreed to him having access to his own son, but now, well I don't have to tell you, do I? It seems you and Phil are planning to restrict his visits.'

'It's Phillip we're thinking of. And we're not restricting Marc's visits; Phillip's getting older, growing up, things change. I've already explained everything to Marc. Phillip doesn't want to be away from home so much during the holidays. He has friends here.'

'He has a home here as well, with his father and sister, and me.'

'Is everything all right between Jenni and Marc?'

'Their relationship has nothing to do with you, Christa.'

'Julie, what is it? We used to be such good friends.'

'That was before you made a fool of my brother.'

'I never made a fool of anyone. And all I said to Marc the last time that we met was that perhaps the visits with Phillip should start to pull back a bit. It's confusing for Phillip. He's growing up now and questioning things. He doesn't want to keep coming to spend time with Marc. He wants to be at home with his friends, but I've already said that.'

'Yes you have. And I'll remind you again if you don't mind, that Phillip has family here too, Christa.'

'This isn't getting us anywhere. I really wanted to ask if you'd heard from Marc and if you knew his plans for Easter. We don't mind Phillip visiting, Phil and I both agree it's ok, but ... he was unhappy the last time. We're not sure that Phillip and Jenni get on. We were wondering if Phillip had done something to upset Jenni, and maybe that's why she lashed out?'

Julie laughed.

'And is that any wonder? Now that you've poisoned Phillip's mind against his step-mother.'

'What? Is that what she said?'

'Jenni hasn't said a word. Marc let me know what was going on, what you'd done; and frankly Christa your sweeter than sugar attitude won't wash anymore.'

'My attitude? Julie it's me, Christa. I was your friend ... I don't understand. And Marc? I don't know what he could have said and I'll not try to second guess, but I can't imagine why he would have said something to you, Julie.'

'I'm his sister, and frankly I'm just pleased that I'm here when he needs someone. We're family, and family look out for each other, and Phillip is part of that family, too.'

'I'm Phillip's mother. I have to make choices.'

'Well perhaps that's where the conversation ends. I can tell you this one piece of news, though, Marc has decided to take things further. He wants to apply for sole custody of Phillip. He doesn't believe that you're a good mother, and as for your husband ... what can I say? Marc doesn't think he's a good role model, not one that he wants for his son. I should think you'll be hearing something soon. And, I'll let Marc know that you've phoned. He'll be wanting to organise things for himself and Phillip over Easter, so he or I will be back in touch. I don't suppose there'll be anything else, will there?'

'No Julie, nothing, thank you.'

I felt as though I'd been hit by a runaway train. Why was Julie so anti me? We'd always got on so well, right from day one. It had to be Marc. Marc must have told her something that had made her see me in a different light, it had to be that. But I knew in my heart that something she had said was very true. And that was that I had probably tricked Marc into giving me a child.

I didn't say anything to Phil when he came in. I wasn't actually sure what I was going to do. He'd have to know eventually of course, but not yet. For now I would keep things to myself.

Marc phoned me the following week. He told me he knew I'd been in touch with Julie; but said that now I was going to hear it straight from him. He wasn't going to be a part- time dad any longer. He had instructed solicitors to act for him and he was going to apply for full custody of Phillip. After all, he said, '*He is my son.*'

I saw red; but I knew I had to stay calm. I couldn't let him know how much he was hurting me.

'This isn't to do with Phillip visiting you, is it? You've planned this all along. My saying that I wanted Phillip's visits to perhaps start to draw back a little was just the catalyst you needed. Well done Marc!'

He answered sarcastically, 'Thank you Christa.'

'Why have you suddenly changed Marc? I thought you still loved me a little, you said you did. And that was only weeks ago. You said you wanted me to meet up with you. You more or less begged me to meet you at *'Our hotel'*. What is the matter with you Marc, do you just like to see me suffer? Is that it? And if none of what you said to me was true, well I can cope with it, but why the hate train? It's not as if I've said you can't see Phillip any more. We've never wanted to stop you seeing Phillip. I don't understand you anymore.'

'Well understand this. I'm not the villain here. No matter how hard you try you're not going to put that one on me.'

'I never thought that Marc, never. And I'm not putting anything on anyone.'

'That's what you're saying now, because as strange as it might seem, and as much as it pains me to say this Christa, I was in love with you, and remember this, I was single; you were the married one. I suppose I got the wrong idea that you had feelings for me. I really believed in you and I also believed that you and my son, the three of us, that one day we'd be a family together. As it is, Phillip knows that I'm his father and yet he treats me as if I'm some distant relative. It's all become a stupid game, and I refuse to play your games anymore.'

I wanted to scream down the phone, *'That's not what we agreed',* but I knew that Marc wasn't altogether wrong. There was a time when I too, thought of the three of us as a family. I tried to remain calm, even though inside I felt as though I was being tied in knots, as though I was being pulled tighter and tighter. And the one doing the pulling, the manipulation? That was Marc. With all the resolve I could muster I let Marc finish his rant, and then I said,

'If that's the way you want it to go, that's your decision, but it's not our decision. Not ours at the beginning Marc, and not mine and Phil's now. And I know things are different, they're different for all of us. You've remarried, you've got Jenni . Me, I've got Phil, and Phil is a good father to Phillip. I'm not pleading Marc, you know he's a good father and in the beginning you seemed to be ok with that. And you and Jenni, I thought you were settled now, on your way to a new life. If things are difficult occasionally, they are in every marriage, nothing is perfect, so ... so don't expect me to come at your beck and call. That's not how it's going to be. We've both made the decisions we have and neither of us can change things now ...'

Marc interrupted.

'I know things have changed, Christa. I don't know when we drifted apart, but I can see that we're where we are now. And we have to take things as they are now and go with them. And right now I believe that Phillip does need to spend more time with me, his natural father. He has to. And personally, I think any court in the land will see it my way.'

'I'll talk to Phil then. I'll tell him exactly how you feel. Maybe we could all meet up and discuss it together. We have to do what's best for Phillip.'

'At least we agree on one thing. You let me know what you decide Christa. I'll wait for your call.'

The phone went dead. Marc had said all he was going to. He left me feeling wretched.

I made myself a cup of coffee and waited for Phillip to come in from school. He was still just nine years old, a bright and bubbly child with lots of friends. The strange thing was the way he did look like Phil. You would automatically take them for father and son; no doubt about it, and that was just what everybody did.

Emotions began to build up inside me and I started to cry. It seemed that everything in my life was in chaos. I felt as though I'd reached the end. I didn't know how much more of this I could take. My life was in ruins.

'We need to talk,' were the words that greeted Phil when he returned later that evening .'Marc's been on the phone.'

'I see. Is there a problem? Is it to do with Easter?'

'It's more than Easter, Phil. It's everything.'

'Well we can't talk now. We'll have to wait until the house is quiet and we're on our own. Now don't worry about anything, it'll all sort itself out; but for the moment we'll just carry on as normal, do all the things we usually do. Now come on, let's have a smile. We'll cope with this.'

I smiled. 'I can always rely on you, can't I, Phil?'

'Always, and do you know what we're going to do?'

'No, what?'

'I'm going to book a table at Mario's and we'll go there to eat. Phillip always loves it there. Go and get your Mum.'

'No, Phil, not tonight, I'm too ... well, this whole thing has worn me out. I just feel shattered.'

Phillip came running into the room.

'Mum, Mum, come quickly, Grandma's not well.'

'What?'

'She's upstairs, we were playing a game and she just fell forward. She won't answer me.'

'Ok, Phillip, you stay here with Mum. I'll go and check on Grandma,' Phil said.

Phil was gone a couple of minutes and then he shouted down the stairs, 'We need an ambulance, Chrissy, get on the phone, now.'

At the hospital Mum was taken to A+E and then on to the coronary care unit. She'd had a heart attack. She was in hospital for the next few days. The good news was that she should make a full recovery.

'Your Mother's very strong, and for her age, remarkable,' a nurse told us.

'We always said she was as tough as old boots,' I said.

When Mum returned home from hospital later the following week, Ken and Bill called in to visit her. I left them alone with Mum. Things hadn't really improved with my brothers since the fiasco at Mum's birthday; but I couldn't turn them away, could I? They were her sons after all. I had to think of Mum.

The talk with Marc hadn't materialised and now Easter was only two weeks away. A decision had to be made. I phoned Julie, who was cold, but there was no ranting. I asked if we were to bring Phillip over for Easter. She was brusque with her reply. Phillip was going to Marc's for the Easter holiday. I knew it had been planned and that Phil and I had agreed to the visit, but I had doubts.

Phil as always, saw the silver lining. He said, 'We've got your Mum to look after. It would probably benefit us all.'

His bright remarks did little to quell my worries.

'They will let us have Phillip back, won't they? Marc wants custody of him. If he gets him down there ... we might not get him back. I don't want him taking my son.'

'Our son, Chrissy. Phillip's our son.'

Phil took me in his arms and held me.

'I love you.'

'I love you too, Phil.'

Mum continued to make good progress and she was soon well enough to take a few steps outside; and thankfully she didn't over do things. Her attitude of 'I'm fine', was one of my worst fears. I didn't want her to start doing too much too soon. I couldn't begin to think of how I would have coped if I'd have had to start reining Mum in, as was usually the case, but this time Mum seemed to be doing everything the doctors had advised. She was a model patient.

The weeks went on and Phil and I eventually got to talk. There'd been no word from Marc about custody and Phillip had returned safe and sound after his Easter visit. Things seemed to be getting back to normal again. And we'd other things to consider with Mum's health issues, and Phillip hadn't once asked us when he could go and visit Marc again, so it seemed the sensible thing to just leave things to settle.

Phil and I talked about a lot of things, things that we'd both been bottling up for the last nine years since Phillip's birth. We realised once everything had been voiced and we'd considered thoroughly what we'd done, and how we'd left everything, just hoping it would be all right, that we'd only been fools to ourselves. We should have had things settled legally right from the start. By doing that, we wouldn't have had all the difficulties now, everyone would have signed to an agreement and known exactly what they were getting. A *gentleman's agreement* was no type of agreement at all. People changed, what they wanted or thought that they wanted, changed. We were finding that out now, to our cost.

Mum wasn't happy that Phillip had gone off to London, to see Marc again, over Easter, but we said that it was Marc doing a favour for us. That he had offered to have Phillip while she recovered from the heart attack. Mum conceded the point but I could tell that she wasn't entirely convinced. Suddenly, I felt the dark waves of depression rush over me. What on earth had I been thinking of in those early years of my marriage? But it wasn't entirely me, was it? Phil hadn't played the marriage game either. He'd left me with no other choice than to make the decision I had, and that decision had led us to where we were today. In one way we were a happy, stable, family unit. In another, we were a loving family, perhaps about to be ripped apart.

It was early May before Marc made any contact. When it came it was just a brief text message asking me to call him.

I phoned Marc the following day, as soon as Phil had left the house. Phil was doing the school run so I only had Mum to worry about. I could manage it. I went to our bedroom, left Mum finishing her breakfast at the kitchen table, never venturing to her my intent.

'Marc?'

'Hi, Christa. About time. You got my message then?'

'Of course. Time's just flown by and Mum's still with us. But don't get angry with me Marc, you did say you'd phone me, that's why I never contacted you. I thought it might not be appropriate.'

'I want to see Phillip. I want him to come down and stay with me for a weekend, perhaps in a week or two, you can let me have dates and I'll sort it out. There's no need for you to come and stay, in fact I don't want you coming down and staying with Julie again. If you did intend to stay, you'd probably be best booking in somewhere. You can drop Phillip off. I'll bring him back; I just wanted to give you warning.'

'I'm not sure Marc. Can it wait a week or two longer? Mum likes him being around and she is his grandmother you know and she has been ill. And what about Jenni? Are you sure she'll want him with you so soon?'

'Christa, he's my son, or had you forgotten? He comes here or I'll start court proceedings. In fact I could say now what's on my mind. You know I've been thinking about this, I have mentioned it before, and the truth of the matter is that I want custody of Phillip – he's mine. He's my son.'

'Marc, I'm his mother. I have to make decisions for him. I don't think this is the right one.'

'You heard me Christa. I mean what I said.'

And with that the phone was put down. I was left looking helplessly into the receiver.

'Are you all right in there? Christine! Christine!'

I must've been numb. I didn't register Mum calling. I put the receiver down and looked at myself in the mirror. I looked dreadful, ashen. There was nothing I could do about it, the way I looked. I would have to face the day as I was, face Mum as I was. I'd already made up my face, but Marc's words had wiped it all away.

I opened the door and was surprised to see Mum standing on the landing.

'Are you ok Mum?'

'I've been tapping on your door and calling your name Christine, not that you noticed. The house could've been burning down. I think you're going deaf.'

'I'm not going deaf Mum, come on, let's go down.'

Mum continued with the conversation on the stairs.

'You never answered when I called you.'

'I'm sorry. I was just going through some papers for Phil. I must've been engrossed. I don't hear a thing when I'm concentrating on something. You know that.'

'Well, as long as you're all right. You had me worried.'

I told Phil everything that night when we were upstairs, alone. He didn't see a problem with letting Phillip go down and stay with Marc, unlike me who still had the mention of custody ringing in my ears, but at the same time, he wasn't keen.

'I don't think we've any need to be worried Chrissy. Marc's not going to go off with Phillip. He'll be safe with him.'

'But after what you said, I thought you were against these visits. I wish we weren't in this mess, because that's what it is, a complete and utter mess.'

Phil looked at me,

'I don't want you going down there, and I think we'll reach a point when Phillip doesn't want to go and stay. He's already said as much, but we've got to try and move on. And we need to keep things on an even keel. We have to be gracious about everything, and we both know that this isn't ideal but it's where we are, and although it's not perfect, I don't think anything in life ever is. And just think what we've gained from everything we've done. We know our marriage is strong and we've a son we both love. And we've no money worries, no debts, no mortgage. Look at those things Chrissy, before you start making up crazy scenarios. Nothing's going to happen to us or to Phillip; we're in a good place, believe me.'

And later, as we lay in bed and Phil put his arms around me, I was glad. Glad because I knew that I needed some comfort and reassurance, and Phil provided both of these things. I also knew that in the past Phil had always been proved right. I knew that he did make the right decisions. I was hoping that he would be right this time.

JUNE 2001

Phillip went to stay with Marc, and as Phil had predicted, there wasn't a problem. There had been no word from Marc since then. He hadn't even phoned to speak to Phillip, which he did occasionally. I lulled myself into a false sense of security, and prayed that everything would stay as it was now. It didn't.

On Saturday June sixteenth Marc finally called. I was in the conservatory with Mum when my mobile began to ring. I recognised the number. I knew it was Marc before he spoke.

'Hello,' I said, 'how are you?'

'Fine, thanks. Is your mum recovered from her heart scare?'

'Yes, she's here now actually; and it was a heart attack.' I turned and looked at Mum, 'She had us all very worried.'

'I think I ought to come over and get this thing sorted out, once and for all. Phillip is my son, after all, and to be honest with you Christa it's as if you're terrified of us, of Jenni and me. I won't stop you from seeing him you know.'

'Well that's a change. Anyway, if you want to meet up perhaps over coffee would be good? '

'I take it you can't talk freely now.'

'No, that's right.'

'I'll ring you back.'

The phone went dead. I put my mobile on the coffee table and sat down. I felt drained. It was unbearable. I felt Mum's eyes drilling through to my very soul. I knew she was going to say something. I decided to get a word in first.

'All right, Mum? Fancy a drink of something cool?'

'I'm fine. Who was that on the phone, Christine?'

'Just an old friend.'

'I see.' Mum went quiet for a moment or two and then said, 'I wondered if it was Phil's cousin, Marc? Just a feeling I had, that's all, what with Phillip staying with him when I came from the hospital and then he went for the weekend didn't he, April, was it?'

'It was Easter, and then he stayed for the weekend a few weeks ago. Marc and his wife Jenni like him to go and stay. It's good of them, don't you think?

'I always thought it was odd, the closeness you had with him, and the way you went down when Phil was working away, you and the baby, and then later you let Phillip go and stay with him on his own. It surprised me really; after all the wait you had to get Phillip. You didn't get pregnant very easily our Christine. I'd have thought you'd have wanted your child with you as much as possible.'

'Marc was good company for me when Phil was away, and Phil knew that his cousin would take care of me and Phillip. And Marc has a daughter, Milly, so it was good for another child to be there.'

'Where's Milly's mother?'

'She was killed in a car accident.'

'Oh. I'm sorry about that. But I can't say I'm sorry that Phillip's spending more time here, with you and Phil. A boy needs to be with his parents, not gallivanting up and down motorways.'

'We made the right choice, then!'

'You did. I think I will have a cool drink if you don't mind Christine; it's getting quite warm in here.'

'I like it out here. I won't be a tick. I'll just get the drinks, any preferences, Mum?'

'Elderflower please.'

When I came back with the drinks I knew Mum was studying me as I walked through the door. I put the drinks down on the table, all the while waiting to see when Mum would speak.

I knew that she would. I knew this because I knew Mum and if there was something she wanted to say, eventually she would. I didn't have to wait for long.

'There's more to this Marc than meets the eye, isn't there? What it is, that I don't know ... Christine?'

'Nothing Mum. I can't think what you mean, there's nothing to know'

'You never were a good liar. I've thought about this for such a long time. At first I thought you were going to leave Phil, but it wasn't that. And then you were expecting Phillip, and then almost immediately Marc appears on the scene. And the strange thing is that for cousins, Phil and Marc always seem distant, friendly yes, yet ... distant. And this Marc, he never came to your wedding. In fact, I'd never heard of him until Phillip was born, and then he's here nearly every God given minute, and if he's not here, then you and Phillip are going off to London visiting. I'm glad it's slackened off a bit, this thing, but I'd be wary off him Christine. I just can't figure him out, and I've tried. He and Phil, they talk to each other and are polite in each other's company; but they don't behave like family, not to my mind anyway. I used to think he came up here to see you. Sometimes the way he looked at you, well it made me wonder, but that was in the early days, and you and Phil were so happy. I mentioned it to your father of course but he told me that it was me; that I was seeing something where there was nothing, but then you were the apple of your father's eye. Ken and Bill didn't have a chance when you came along. They both had their noses pushed out of joint, but that's another story. Anyway, to get back to what I was saying, this Marc, when I've seen him lately he seems detached, as if he's got a lot on his mind, and that's what I've been mulling over, and I'd be pleased if you would just tell me what it is that's going on. I know there's something wrong. The real picture isn't what's being painted, why?'

'There's nothing really to tell, Mum. There's really not much that you haven't already said.' I paused for a moment before carrying on. I felt that now was the right time. Mum had to know about Phillip eventually and for whatever reason, I don't know ... I was going to tell her now. Now was definitely the right time.

'You've gone quiet Christine.'

'I was just thinking about something. Something that I perhaps should have told you a long time ago. Something that I hope won't hurt you or the way you feel about me as your daughter, or Phillip. You see you're right, Mum; Marc isn't Phil's cousin, but he is Phillip's Dad. You were bound to ask me outright one of these days. And for some strange reason I feel better now that you know.'

'I knew there was something, I knew there was. You cheated on your husband, then, deceived Phil? I'm surprised Phil's been so understanding all this time. I'd never have thought that of you Christine, never. I don't know what your father would have made of it all. All I can say is that it's a good job he's not here to know.'

'It's not as black and white as you're painting it, Mum. There are some things that I might never be able to tell you. It needs a lot of explaining and I'm not going to do that without Phil being here.'

'That's fair enough. I'll say no more.'

'Thanks Mum, and one more thing, not a word of this to Phillip. He knows that Marc's his real dad, and we've never had a problem with it; but he also knows that to all intents and purposes, Phil's his dad, and that's how we want it. Please promise that you won't say a word to him.'

Phillip came in from school and was straight off to a friend's house. He and Sam were busy counting the days off to the end of term in July. Sam's parents had asked if Phillip could go with them for a week's holiday in Somerset. Phil and I had agreed and Phillip was really looking forward to it, saving every spare bit of money he was given and not spending his pocket money as soon as he received it, which he could usually do without giving it a moment's thought.

When Phillip and Sam returned to school in the September they would be in year six. It would be their final year at junior school. My son was growing up. The time had flown by. The baby I had wanted so desperately would soon be stepping out into a new phase of his life. It seemed almost impossible to believe.

I had never had any problems with Phillip. I think I was just lucky because some of the other mums at school used to tell me what scrapes their children had got into. Some of the tales were quite hair-raising. Phillip was a good lad and within reason mostly did as he was told. If I had asked him to be home by six-thirty, I knew he would be. I had never had to go searching for him or knocking on doors to get him to come home. At school he rarely got into any bother. Homework was sometimes late, but that was about all anyone had any real complaint about. When I looked at Phillip I counted my blessings. How lucky I was.

As soon as Phillip was out of the door and away to Sam's house, I phoned Phil. I asked him if he could be home within the half hour. I explained briefly about the call from Marc and what I'd said to Mum.

Phil walked in the door twenty minutes later. He tried to raise a smile, but didn't quite manage it. He looked worried. Mum and I were sitting in the lounge. Phil acknowledged Mum first.

'Hello Mum. Enjoying the sun?'

'I am ... but you and Christine have got to get things sorted out. You've got yourselves into a right hornets' nest, haven't you? Christine's told me a lot of what's gone on. Marc's got a point you know, he is Phillip's dad. And I don't think you can go on like you have been going on for much longer. It's called burying your head in the sand. And Phillip's growing up. And it's all right saying that, *Phillip knows Marc's his 'real' dad.* But he doesn't really treat him as such, does he? And that's not fair, either. I was telling Christine this afternoon that she was always good at getting things her own way. I know you'll probably want to deny it Christine, but nevertheless, it's true. You could just do with thinking back a few years, before any of you were married and it was you and the boys at home. This wife of yours, Phil, well she made her brothers' lives a misery at times. What with her tormenting and remarks she made, and she got away with it a lot of the time because of her dad. Her dad doted on her and so she became used to having her own way. I tried not to let her get away with too much, and if her dad wasn't there she sometimes got the sharp side of my tongue, the little madam. But you're adults now, the pair of you and believe me Phil, it's time to start acting like it. You need to get things out in the open. You've done well to keep your secret safe for so long, but let it be a good thing in the long run if it has an airing. You don't want to let any gossip or tittle-tattle start. Phillip will only end up in the middle of it, and that's not fair. It's better that he hears everything from you two, the people he calls Mum and Dad, than from outsiders who just want to throw their two penn'orth in the ring and see how far it goes. I know from what Christine's told me that you've already done all this, or thought you had, but none of it was set in place legally. It was a friendly arrangement, and such arrangements can easily fall down, as you're finding out now. I'll not say I'm sorry for the two of you, but Phillip's my grandson. It's him I'm thinking of. Anyway, I've said my piece. I'll leave you two to talk things over before Phillip comes home. And if there's only one piece of advice I can give you, after all I've just said, let it be this; after you've talked things over, make an appointment and go and get some advice from a solicitor.'

By the time Phillip came in Phil and I felt we had been talking for two days, not two hours. We both felt exhausted by it all.

'Why isn't tea ready?' Phillip asked as he stuck his head round the door. 'I could've stayed longer at Sam's if I'd known.'

I'd never even thought about preparing a meal for us; circumstances had overtaken everything. Phil got up from the sofa.

'Tea isn't ready because we're all going out for a meal. Go and get changed and then you can tell your Gran to get her glad rags on too,' Phil said.

Phillip's face lit up.

'Great,' he said. 'Going out on a school night.'

JULY 2001

We went to see a solicitor as Mum had advised. And of course, she was right. It was definitely the right thing to do. We had to know what would go for or against us. It was only wise to be prepared. I wondered why none of us had raised the subject of putting everything on a legal footing earlier. But I suppose back then that none of us had thought about where the path we had taken would lead us. And I know that all I had wanted was a child. I suppose naively, that I thought once I was pregnant the job was done. I should have realised that it was only the beginning, and back then, in those far off days before Phillip was born, none of us knew how feelings would grow and change over the years. We did just think it would *'be all right.'*

So, taking Mum's advice turned out to be the best thing we could have done. It seemed that even if Marc did go ahead and apply for custody of Phillip, there were a lot of factors that were in our favour. I was pleased with what the solicitor had to say and we both came out of the office feeling much brighter. We now had someone on our side.

I hadn't heard from Marc in the interim and it was difficult to determine what his next move would be. I knew I wouldn't be phoning him. I would leave it up to him to make the next move. I just wondered when that would be, and that left me in a permanent state of flux. One step forward and two steps back.

AUGUST 2001

I didn't have much longer to wait. By the end of the first week in August Marc had phoned. He said he was coming up to see us the following weekend. He asked if we'd be available but the tone of his voice told me that he wouldn't accept '*no*' for an answer. I told him we'd be in whenever he cared to call. I also told him that Mum knew who he was and that there was no point playing the game any longer. It would be best, I told him, if from now on we all stopped trying to pretend. After all Phillip knew he was his real father, so what else mattered?

I knew that I would never and could never, do anything that I believed would hurt Marc. I had loved him once; truly, deeply, honestly and he was the father of my son. And my son was the person who mattered more to me than anything else in the world. And feelings do run deep, so, despite everything that had ever happened a tiny part of me still loved Marc, and always would. And that was the odd thing; you see I was no longer *in love* with him. I no longer wanted him. That was all finished; over and done with. And when I looked at Phillip it was Phil who I saw looking back at me. It was as if Marc had had nothing to do with him, nothing at all. Phil and Phillip were the two people my life revolved around, and that was the way it was going to stay.

The following weekend when Marc arrived at the house I was a bag of nerves. I didn't know what to expect. When Marc's car pulled up outside the house I watched and waited; waited to see if Jenni was with him. She wasn't. Marc was alone. That at least was a relief to me. I just couldn't help the feeling inside me, and the thought that Jenni had a lot more to do with the way Marc was acting and behaving now. It was right that she wasn't here, that she had stayed away. What we three had to discuss had nothing at all to do with her. Nothing.

The doorbell rang. I stayed where I was, in the lounge. Phil squeezed my hand as he went past me and into the hall. I listened as Phil opened the door, and then I heard Marc say *'Hello'* and then I heard the door close. Marc smiled as he came into the lounge. Phil followed and sat next to me. Somewhat woodenly I said to Marc,

'Take a seat.' Marc turned slightly and sat down in one of the chairs that was placed directly facing us.

'Is Phillip home? I haven't seen him in such a long time.'

'He's gone to a birthday party, a friend's ...'

'Convenient,' Marc replied, cutting in before I had time to finish the sentence.

I felt myself getting hot. If this was the start of the discussion what would I be like when it was over and it was time for Marc to leave? I paused and took a deep breath to compose myself.

'Not convenient,' I said, 'the truth,' He's been on holiday in Somerset for a week with a friend, and today is his friend's birthday. Sam's parents have taken Phillip and several other boys ten pin bowling.'

'Ok, ok. I was just hoping to see him today, that's all, and you never mentioned anything, I just assumed ...'

Now it was my turn to cut in, and I did so without allowing Marc a second to continue.

'I didn't think it mattered that Phillip wouldn't be here, and if you stay long enough Phillip might be home. I've already made coffee,' I said, 'I'll bring it through, or would anyone prefer tea?'

'Coffee's fine,' Marc replied.

Phil just nodded. I went through to the kitchen and returned with the tray. When I sat down Phil said,

'From the most recent phone calls you've made Marc, it seems that things between you and Chrissy have become rather heated. I hope we can have a grown up discussion today; keep everything on an even keel, no raised voices or lost tempers. I agree with you Marc that this whole thing has to be sorted out and the sooner the better. And I know that whatever feelings we have about this and how it has affected our lives we must keep one point central, and that's the need to do what's right.'

'I've not come here to cause trouble,' Marc replied.

I just sat, coffee cup in hand and looked at the two men. I had loved both of them, but now I was in love with only one of them, and that was Phil. I decided I couldn't stay silent any longer. Whether it was for right or wrong, I had to say my piece, and nothing was going to stop me. I know that Phil and I had discussed what we would say at this meeting, as I was sure Marc and Jenni would have done. And I knew that Phil's advice had been for me to stay calm, to keep Marc on side, but I guess my mother knew me too well. Hadn't she said only last week that I always got what I wanted? Hadn't she more or less told Phil to rein me in? She had. And I'd been there and listened, and I knew for the most part that what Mum had said was true. Even so, I just couldn't stop myself.

I felt Phil look at me as I turned and looked directly at Marc. Phil questioned me with his eyes, saying nothing and I could tell that he was imploring me to do the same. It wasn't going to work. I began.

'Can I just say something before we carry on? Phillip's my son. I'm his mother. I gave birth to him and I think he should stay with me, with us, with Phil and me. We're the only family he's ever known, really. And his grandmother lives with us now, and they are both really attached to each other. They are really exceptionally close, and the bond has strengthened since my father died. For Phillip to be taken away could cause him serious emotional problems. He's growing up. He'll be going to senior school soon and then have all the upheaval and trauma that can go with that.

And he is sensitive. Any change coming along now in the way that he lives and where he lives ... it will just cause untold problems. I'm sure of that and I won't allow it to happen. And you Marc, you say you're his father, well behave like his father and don't disrupt what for Phillip is a happy and stable family life.'

'Pretty speech, Christa. But don't forget that I'm his father,' Marc replied. I must have some part in his life; some say in any decisions that affect him. And that's all that I'm asking for. I don't think that my request is unreasonable, not at all. I want to play some part more in his life than I play now. I want to be relevant and not someone who just appears every now and again like some benevolent uncle figure. That's not what I am and that's not what I want. I don't believe it's fair the way things have gone. To be honest I feel as though I'm being marginalised. I feel that each time I ask to see my son that you'll come up with some flimsy excuse and that I'm supposed to bend to your every whim. I want more access to *my* son.'

I was seething. I knew that what Marc was saying, was in some ways true. But I couldn't give in, not now. I laid down the markers. I was setting out my claim as I saw it and I wasn't bothered what Marc thought or felt.

My voice was raised, slightly, more to make a point than out of any real anger towards Marc. I wanted him to realise that he couldn't have things his way, that Phillip was my son, and that I knew what was best for him.

'That's not what we agreed. The three of us, right from the start ... well you knew how it was going to be Marc and you can't just start changing your mind now because you think it will suit you better.'

'No, what's not right Christa, is that you changed your mind. You promised me that you'd marry me, but eh, look, it never happened.'

Phil stood up and intervened. Looking first to me and then to Marc.

'Come on, we know what we said at the time and that's almost ten years ago now; and we would still go along with that to a degree I think, although I personally feel that Phillip is my son, whether I'm his biological father or not. I'm named as the father on his birth certificate and Chrissy is my wife. What I don't think is in any way fair is if you, Marc, start trying to threaten us with claims that you want sole custody of Phillip and insinuate that I'm not a fit person to be a father. That Chrissy and I, that we're not suitable as people to be parents to our own child; that we can't be a family. I will dispute that with every breath in my body.'

'I know when we've met up over the years you've seemed ok, but you must admit that your past lifestyle was hardly squeaky clean. You didn't seem to think much of Christine then.'

'That's all in the past, done with; finished. I'm a husband to my wife and a father to my son.'

Marc countered, 'But you're *not* his father, are you? Phillip's my son.'

The whole discussion was becoming unbearable. We were getting nowhere. I began to cry. Phil at once put his arms around me.

'Hey, come on,' he said, 'We can sort this out. It'll be all right.'

'I don't want to upset you Christa, but this thing needs to be brought out into the open,' Marc said.

Through my tears I replied to Marc's last cutting comments, I had to.

'This *thing* that you say needs bringing out into the open. This *thing* you're talking about is our son, Marc! He's our son, and I don't know about you, but Phil and I happen to love him and care about him. We want the best for him.'

'And I don't? Don't be stupid Christa. Why else would I want him to come and live with me, permanently?'

'I don't know,' I replied. 'I don't know; no more than I ever thought you could be so heartless and cruel and treat me as you are doing. I suppose it could be that you want to get back at me, at me and Phil because things haven't gone the way you'd have liked them to; because I changed my mind about marrying you.'

'Me heartless and cruel? I don't think so. Take a look at yourself Christa, a long look. You're not little Miss Perfect you know. And when we get custody of Phillip, Jenni and me, we will offer him a better life in London than he has here with you. That's one thing I will promise.'

'There's nothing wrong with the life he has here. It's where he goes to school. It's where his friends are,' I said.

'Maybe,' Marc said. 'But I think you're short changing him, that's all. What he has here is hardly the life he would have if he was living with me permanently.'

I could see Phil becoming more and more agitated. He turned to face Marc.

'Now, leave it there. There's nothing wrong with where we live or the way we look after Phillip and bring him up. He's a happy well-adjusted child. We don't want to say, any of us, things that we could regret. Marc, just lay your cards on the table. What is it exactly that you want?'

'I'd have thought that was pretty obvious from the conversations I've had on the phone with Christa. I want sole custody of Phillip, of my son. I want him to come and live with myself and Jenni. Jenni thinks the world of Phillip and she would make a wonderful mother; and the tragedy is, well ... I won't beat about the bush; Jenni can't have children.'

'So we should all feel sorry for Jenni because she can't have children? Well she's not having my son! He's my son, not Jenni's, and to be honest with you Marc she doesn't like him. It got to such a point at one time, if you remember, or maybe you just choose to forget, but it got to such a point that Phillip was almost begging me not to let him visit with you again! I thought that you'd have remembered that, after all you phoned me and had to bring Phillip home a couple of days early. I wonder if

Jenni, the marvellous mother figure has forgotten it as well? Well let me tell you, just for the record, that I haven't.'

'You don't have to bring all that up again, Christa. That was in the past. I know when I brought Phillip back he did say that he didn't want to visit me if Jenni was there because there'd been a misunderstanding, but Jenni was upset. And, she gets angry when she's upset. That's why she might have said some things that she'd regret later. And she does have regrets, she's not made of stone you know, she does have a heart. She's horrified now to even think that she could have said such things in front of him. She wouldn't do anything to upset Phillip, not intentionally. And you Christa, you may be able to lie and bluff to your husband, but can anyone really believe what you say? Look how you lied to me.'

'What I'm telling you is true. And you can't deny it. You're not turning things round to suit your own ends because it won't wash, Marc. And your wife is not playing house or happy families or whatever else you want to call it with my son.'

Marc got up. His coffee cup was still full.

'I think I'd better leave. You'll be hearing from my solicitor, you realise that?'

'Just try it Marc, just try it. And yes, I think it is time that you left.' The words almost choked me, but I said them and be done with it. I heard the front door bang closed, and then the opening and closing of a car door. There was a screech of tyres as he pulled away. We had been talking but nothing had really been said.

Nothing that moved us any further on. I knew that Marc hadn't been bluffing when he said that we'd hear from his solicitor. It would just be a matter of time. I felt sick when Marc left. Sick and shattered.

'We'd better start planning things. Phil said. 'It looks like your mum's advice, as usual, will be proved to have been right.'

'It usually is,' I replied.

Over the next few weeks we received various letters from Marc's legal team. He'd done exactly as he'd promised he would. Could we ever have expected anything less from this man?

I was feeling wretched all the time. I had no interest in anything. I was just living from day to day; from letter to letter. In one of the letters I had notice that, 'Marcus Blake wished to prove his paternity of Phillip'. It would mean subjecting Phil and Phillip to the giving of a swab. Not a terrible thing to have to do, but I wondered what Phillip would make of it?

I explained the whole process to Phillip, told him what would happen, and as usual, he just took everything in his stride.

Phil didn't have any problems with it either. He said that we should go along with it, keep everybody sweet. He knew what it would prove, as did I. We both knew that Marc was definitely Phillip's father.

SEPTEMBER 2001

In a few weeks it would be mine and Phil's wedding anniversary. I knew Phil would hold on to the traditions that had become ours. The little rituals that every couple has; and that no one else knows about. It becomes a secret between them, and that is just the way it should be.

I knew that a few weeks further on it would be Phillip's birthday. I couldn't even begin to think of planning a party or even asking Phillip what he'd like to do. I was just waiting for the next hurdle that dropped itself in front of my path, the next obstacle that I would have to deal with. The next communication from Marc and his *legal team.*

It's a good job Phil stayed calm and solid through it all. He was just what I needed. I was like a piece of wire that's been pulled too tightly. I felt as though at any minute I might snap. My whole being was at breaking point. I couldn't eat. I'd lost weight. Mum was worried. She didn't want me neglecting myself, and forthright as ever, she didn't waste any time in telling me so.

'You've got to think of Phillip. He needs a mum. He needs you. You must stay strong for him. You're no use to him as you are. Look at yourself Christine, you're wearing yourself out. You can't carry on as you are doing and not expect there to be any detrimental consequences. You're travelling on a downhill path, you've got to try and pull yourself together.' And then she added, as an afterthought, 'I am on your side Christine. I couldn't bear to lose my grandson, and I know what it would do to you if that were to happen, if you were to lose your son ... but, you do know that in most of these cases, the child does end up staying with the mother.'

'Is that right?'

'Yes. I believe so; so just stay strong and focus on that.'

I knew she was right. And Mum had always been a strong one. Me, I just got through, I coped. Other people, outsiders, thought I was strong. I didn't tend to give anything away; I put on an act. But that was only to a degree. If they could've seen inside me, they would've seen a different person. They would've realised that I was at breaking point, and that for me, wasn't a nice place to be.

Phil was worried about me as well, but he was less forthright than Mum. He just concentrated on the practicalities.

'I know we're going through a tough patch; but I know we'll come out the other side stronger for it. I know that everything will be ok. It'll all work out in our favour, I know it will. Just trust me on this one, Chrissy. You see, I can cope with you being on edge and wanting to turn away from everything; but what I can't cope with is you not eating. You're losing weight, Chrissy; your mum's right, and if this carries on you'll have to make an appointment to see the doctor, because ... even though you're not ill now, you soon will be. You just can't carry on like this. Just look at what you're doing to yourself. Nothing's worth making yourself ill for.'

'This isn't nothing Phil. This is Phillip we're talking about. This is Phillip I'm worrying about. I can't stand by and let him be taken from me.'

'And neither can I. Neither will I. And I don't believe it's going to come to that. Believe me.'

I knew what Phil was saying was the truth; I knew that Mum and Phil were both right in what they were saying; it just didn't make things any easier. Phil looked at me, questioningly.

'Well?' he said.

'Let's just get the paternity test done, get the swabs out of the way first, and Phillip's birthday; that's my next project. After that I'll see how I'm feeling. But hopefully I should be feeling better by then.'

'Promise you'll see the doctor if nothing changes?'

'I promise.'

Marc remained a little hostile towards us. The phone calls were brief and were usually no more than updating us and perhaps having a chat with Phillip. Phillip didn't like these calls from Marc. He complained that often they were just, *'Loads of questions'*. It had reached a point where the only contact that was in any way civil was usually in the form of a solicitor's letter. These letters too, were brief and often demanding, but we coped with them. Marc had got his teeth fixed firmly into us now and he wasn't in the mood for giving up. At times I barely recognised the man I believed I had been so in love with. And it was obvious now that he no longer had any feelings for me. Everything seemed to be on a purely business footing. He wanted Phillip, that was all there was to it. I was merely thankful at the moment that Marc wasn't demanding extra visits from Phillip. At least my son was with me, for the time being.

I began to wonder if Marc had used me during the time of our affair. Had he carefully planned everything all along to end like this? After all, I had told him right from the start that I was married, and yet he still pursued me. Sometimes I truly believed that he had done everything he possibly could to keep me with him. Perhaps he had seen me as a good mother figure for Milly. It was probable of course; but then all things are. It wasn't a one way street either. I too was guilty. After all, hadn't I deliberately gone out looking for a suitable man to father a child for me; a child that my husband refused to give me. Well, yes, I had. But I had also chosen someone I could love, and even though there were doubts, I did believe that Marc had also once loved me.

If Marc had used me, then what I believed was right and good about our affair and our time together would become a lie. I didn't want it to be like that. I didn't, but the whole thing was becoming a weight I felt unable to bear. I was thankful for Phil and the love and support he offered me every day. Without it I wouldn't have been able to carry on. I know that. I would have been unable to cope. I would have given up and probably agreed to everything that Marc wanted; even if that included giving up Phillip.

It was just before Phillip's birthday in October that the letter arrived. The letter we had been expecting and dreading with equal measure. The result of the paternity test. Phil and I always knew what the outcome would be, of course. But to see it there in black and white, it cut us both right through to the quick. Funny, isn't it, how the truth can hurt so much, even when it's expected. It was 99% accurate it said. The one percent wasn't worth bothering about. Phillip could be no one else's son but Marc's.

Another letter arrived with it. Marc had advised his solicitor that he wanted to apply for custody of his son. He had set the wheels in motion. It didn't feel as if they would ever stop turning.

Phillip's birthday party was at a leisure centre in town; five-a-side football and burgers afterwards. He loved it. There was one more surprise in store for us that afternoon, something Phil and I hadn't planned for. I'd mentioned to Marc what we were doing for Phillip's party the last time we'd spoken on the phone. Marc knew the leisure centre as he'd been there with Phillip when he'd come up to visit the two of us in the early days.

I never dreamed that he'd show up today though, I had just mentioned it out of courtesy. I was keeping him 'onside' as Phil called it. Phillip soon spotted him. I instantly wondered how Phillip would react. As usual, he took it in his stride.

'It's Marc! He's made it to my party,' Phillip said, and his face lit up as he caught sight of Marc as soon he appeared in the viewing area.

I was glad Mum had stayed at home. This visit wouldn't have gone down well.

'Wouldn't miss it Phillip. Wouldn't miss your birthday for the world.'

I didn't know whether Marc meant the words he had just spoken, but I hoped for our son's sake that he did. Marc looked across at me and smiled. I felt like I had just died inside.

My worries were however, unfounded. It was all very civilised. Marc wasn't awkward or demanding. He was polite and the afternoon went by just as though it was a regular visit that we had planned. In fact at one point he and Phil were chatting like old mates, like they used to. It made me think that Jenni really had had more to do with Marc's change of attitude than he would ever admit. I wanted to say something, to ask, but I bit my tongue. What would have been the point?

Marc left after having a burger and watching Phillip blow out the candles on his cake. He hugged him and then he was on his way.

'I'd better make a move now, it's a good two and a half hours run from here, and I'm in the office first thing. I've got a new project I'm hoping to secure and I need to do some preparation work this evening when I get back.'

'I hope it goes well,' I said, 'drive safely and thanks for coming down.' And they weren't just empty words. I meant them, every one.

Marc pushed an envelope into my hand,

'This is for Phillip. It's a cheque. I didn't know what he'd want so I thought that this was best.'

'He'd have been happy with anything, a bar of chocolate. It wouldn't have mattered.'

'Can't see me doing that somehow, can you? Anyway, you'll know the kind of thing he likes and you can go together and choose, or if he wants he can bank it, I suppose. Saving is never a bad thing.'

'That's true,' I said.

'Party's over now,' Phil said when we arrived home. 'How are you feeling?'

He knew I'd found this afternoon a trial for all that it went well and I still wasn't feeling any better.

'I was surprised when Marc came but it wasn't so bad. You two actually seemed to be getting along ok at one point when I looked across at you.'

'We've always got on, not always agreed, but always got on.'

'Anyway, that doesn't answer my question, how are you feeling?'

'As always.'

'And will you keep your promise?'

'What's that?'

'Don't pretend you don't know. The promise, the doctor's appointment.'

'Oh, that.'

'Yes, oh that.'

'Probably.'

'No, not probably, that's not good enough; it's definitely.'

I looked at Phil and smiled .'I'll phone on Monday, promise.'

I knew I couldn't hold off any longer. Mum and Phil, they were right. I needed help. I needed something else as well. I needed to know that I could keep my son with me, with us, but that was going to take a little longer to sort out, to reach its conclusion.

I phoned the surgery and made a doctor's appointment for the following Friday. I told myself that if I was feeling any better by then, that I could always cancel.

Friday morning arrived. I felt wretched. I waited in the reception area at the surgery and felt as though I were about to receive the death penalty with no chance of a reprieve. I couldn't have felt any worse than I did that morning.

My name came up on the call board. The tick-a-tape red lettering telling me that I was to go through to room six, Dr Ellis's room. Dr Ellis listened patiently and then got me to lie on the couch where she began to poke and prod at my body. She wanted blood and urine samples taking and she sent me there and then straight through to the nurse.

'These blood tests, you can ring the surgery for the results in five days, but make sure you call after three p.m.,' the nurse said, 'but from the urine sample it looks like good news. When was your last period?'

'I don't remember. My mum's been ill, a heart attack and various other things are going on at home at the moment, family problems, not at home, not with my home life but everything's been very hectic and I've lost track.'

'Don't you mark the date in your diary?'

'Usually. But I've been too busy.'

'Would you mind checking?'

'You don't think ... No! It can't be.'

'I think it is Mrs Beacham.'

I walked home in a dream, a daze. I would tell Phil first, of course. But I'd have to wait until he got home. The next few hours would be awkward. I was actually dying to tell somebody, anybody. I felt really happy at the good news and yet at the same time wondered how I could get through the afternoon without giving anything away either to my mum or Phillip.

'What did the doctor say?' Mum asked.

'Nothing much. I've just been overdoing things a bit, and worrying.'

'I'll say. Who did you see?'

'Dr Ellis.'

'Oh, And did she mention your weight? There's hardly a pick on you. I'll have to make you some of my stews. The weather will be getting colder soon; it'll be the weather for warming, old fashioned meals. That's what you need my girl, something to build you up again.'

'Thanks Mum. That'd be really good.'

'So she didn't say anything much at all then.'

'Not a lot to say. The doctor sent me through to the nurse and she's taken blood. I have to ring in a few days for the results.'

'Why have they done that, what do they think it is? They must've said something Christine.'

'They didn't. We'll just have to wait until the results are back. I suppose they want to see if I'm anaemic, that's why they've taken blood. And you've been telling me for weeks I'm not looking after myself. I guess everything's finally caught up with me.'

'Well it's true. You're not looking after yourself. I keep telling you, but you don't seem to want to listen. I've known for weeks there's something wrong.'

'Yes, well I've been to the doctor's now, so hopefully in a day or two we'll get to find out what's the matter with me. I don't think it'll be anything nasty, so don't you go worrying yourself Mum. With everything else that's going on, I need to be able to rely on you.'

Mum smiled. I wondered what she'd be like when I finally told her my news?

Phil phoned to say he'd be late.

'You'd all better eat without me. I've got to go and see one of our new contractors, we've been let down on a job and I've got to go and try to smooth things over. I won't be too late and I'll sort myself out when I come in. I'd better go now.'

'Do you want me to save you something?'

'If it's not too much trouble.'

'It won't be.' I paused. I couldn't help myself from asking him one more thing, even though I could tell from Phil's voice that he was in a hurry.

'Don't you want to ask me anything?' I said.

'I'm sorry Chrissy, you've been to the doctor haven't you, everything ok?'

'Fine, nothing to worry about.'

'That's good. I'll speak to you later, love you.'

Phil was later than he anticipated and as keen as I was to tell him the news, I didn't dive straight in as soon as he walked through the door, although it was what I wanted to do. That pleasure went to Mum. As soon as she heard the door she was out of the conservatory and into the hall in a flash.

'Christine's been to the doctor's. They can't tell her anything for a few days. They've taken blood. Think she might be anaemic. And you, you'll be there next, at the doctor's. You look all in my lad. The pair of you need to take care of yourselves. Anyway, that's all I've to say. I'll go and read some more of my book. Leave you two to sort yourselves out.'

I put Phil's dinner in the microwave and heated it through. It was steak and ale pie, and although I knew that the microwave would make the pastry soft, I reckoned that once the gravy was added, it wouldn't really matter. He would be more than thankful that there was a hot meal there for him. Phil didn't remember to ask me anything about my day when he came in. He looked shattered and I told him so. Repeating what my Mum had just said.

I'd waited all day with my news, a little while longer wasn't going to make any difference at all, but as I sat watching him eat, I felt that I might burst at any moment.

'Thanks for waiting up for me. That pie was delicious, worth being late for. That doesn't sound right, but you know what I mean.'

I laughed. 'I know what you mean.'

'It's been an awful day. I couldn't keep up with everything that was going on. I'd no sooner sorted out one problem than another one came out to get me. Anyway, I've sorted the problem out with the contractor and as long as his workmen are on site in the morning, there's no serious damage done, but we could do without it, that's all.'

Phillip was in bed and Mum was sitting in the conservatory reading. She said she liked the quietness in there. I think it was that you could see the garden from all sides. And even though the nights were drawing in now, the lighting in the garden cast shadows over the plants and shrubs. It made everything seem so serene. I popped my head round the door and said goodnight. Mum put her book down and looked up.

'It's not often I'm up after you,' she said laughing.

Phil and I went up to bed.

'Had anything from Marc and his team in the post today?' Phil asked.

'No', I replied. 'Nothing new, but I expect there must be dozens of solicitor's letters out there somewhere in the ether.'

We never discussed anything about the custody cloud hanging over our heads in front of Phillip. No point in pursuing the matter until you had to; and since the swabs had been taken, there hadn't been any more questions asked. Life generally, at home, was good. Phil and I were both thankful for small mercies.

Phil didn't pursue his line of questioning, there was no mention from him at all of me and my appointment at the doctor's. I felt as though I had a permanent smile fixed on my face. I looked at him. Willing him to start a conversation. I knew he was shattered after his long day's work, but I had to say something. I couldn't wait any longer, and definitely not 'til morning.

'Chrissy, what is it? You look, well you look; is there something you want to tell me?'

'I thought you might have asked me how I was. I've had the doctor's appointment today, had you forgotten?' I said.

'Sorry, Chrissy. It slipped my mind, and then your mum was on to me as soon as I came in. She said that you've been worrying too much, which isn't surprising I suppose, anyway, you tell me, how did you go on?'

'Well, all right really, nothing to worry about, that's the good news, but there is one thing I need to tell you and something that I probably should mention to Marc, as well.'

'But you're ok, though, aren't you?'

'Yeah, of course, but there is something else, it's not just the worry that's affecting me, Phil, it's you, you're going to be a dad, sometime in April.'

'What, me?'

'Yes, you. I guess with everything else I never thought of what was really obvious.'

'No, and your mum, she doesn't know yet, you haven't told her?'

'No. She just thinks I want feeding up.'

'And Phillip?'

'No, he doesn't know. I wanted to tell you first.' Phil looked at me.

'I've always loved you, you know.'

'I know.'

'This is fantastic news.'

To say Mum was pleased was the biggest understatement of the year. She was ecstatic. 'I knew there was something,' she said. 'I've been dreaming of eggs.'

I thought it was only fair to let Marc know and Phil agreed; particularly as Marc had let me know about their problems; about Jenni. It was funny, but I felt strangely sorry now, for them, and particularly for her.

I'd tried so hard for my son, and now I was being given more. And all this at a time when things had seemed so awful; so awful for all of us.

And here I was being given hope. In a few months Phil and I would have another child, our second child.

It seemed life was a roller-coaster. A never ending series of twists and turns to test your life skills. Was anybody ever prepared enough?

It took a lot of courage to get me to finally phone Marc, even though I knew it had to be done. I wondered how he'd take things. I didn't want Marc to think I was gloating. I definitely wasn't.

He seemed ok about everything when I eventually made the call, pleased for us, in fact; and he said he would tell Jenni later, when she arrived in from work, then he added,

'She's really throwing herself into work at the moment. She's been like this since the last miscarriage, that was when she was given the news, the news that she couldn't have children. But you Christa, you know what it's like to desperately want a child.'

Of course I did, but our paths, Jenni's and mine were totally different. I wasn't unable to have children. Jenni was in an unenviable position. I thought of all the times I'd thought about her poisoning Marc's mind against me. Of the time she'd upset Phillip so much that he had to come home from Marc's early. Perhaps all the time she was seeing in Phillip the child she wanted, the child who wasn't hers. Perhaps that was the reason she persecuted me, through Marc. Maybe I had read her wrong all along. I couldn't help that now, but maybe there was a lesson to be learned. I vowed to try and like Jenni, to try and see things from her point of view. I wondered how she would feel when Marc told her my news? I hoped she wouldn't find it too upsetting.

Marc was happy for us, and I could tell that was genuine. And I was telling the truth when I told him that I was saddened to hear their news. What a situation to be in?

I put the phone down. I'd been honest and that's all that I could do.

A few weeks later we had a call from our solicitor's office. When could we go in? Mr Graham wanted to see us urgently.

I instantly went on the defensive. But the receptionist wouldn't say *why* they needed us to go in urgently.

'I wonder what's brought this on? Marc wasn't so bad when I told him about the baby. In fact he seemed genuinely pleased.'

Phil was more pragmatic. 'Let's just get there. We'll find out soon enough.'

We were however bracing ourselves for more bad news. That's what solicitors do, don't they? Prepare you and help you through the worst.

We took the next available date they had, the following day, ten-thirty. We didn't want to delay things unnecessarily.

'Sit down, Mr and Mrs Beacham.'

Our solicitor was Mr Graham, the youngest of the partners, and someone whose name bore no resemblance at all to the name above the door of the office.

He continued, 'I've a letter here from the firm of Mr N. Stones who was acting for Mr Marcus Blake. I am to inform you that Mr Marcus Blake wishes to stop all proceedings regarding the custody claim. He won't be taking matters any further.'

'Does he say why?' Phil asked.

'Not in any detail. This letter just states the fact that he's had a change of mind. That's it. But I thought you'd be relieved to know. I can imagine that it will be a weight off your shoulders.'

That was an understatement to say the least. Phil and I went home with lighter hearts and we were happier than we had been in months. We were a family again. A true family. A growing family.

The way was clear now for us to let Phillip in on the news that he was going to be a big brother. We didn't delay.

DECEMBER 2001

Christmas was a wonderful affair. My bump was still small enough to not be causing me any major problems. Mum and Phillip were a good help regarding the preparation on the day; and Christmas, however low key you make it is always a busy time. Phil, well he did just what he always did at Christmas; he went to town. There were lights and decorations in every room and in and on every available space. I had been worried as things hadn't really settled down within our family. Yes, the unpleasantness between ourselves and Marc was over with, but my brothers and their families, they hardly visited, and when they did come to see Mum, well then the conversation turned to her house and family finances and how she would be better off selling if she was going to be staying with me and Phil. Phil and I just let it wash over us, as long as Mum was ok, then that was all that mattered, and her house? We checked on it, regularly. We made sure everything was in order and kept the garden tidy. Everything was under control. And Phil? Phil remained adamant that it was just going to be a Christmas *for us;* none of the wider family were to be invited.

I accepted it. Ken and Bill hadn't offered us an invitation either. I just wanted to enjoy the day; and hoped especially that Mum would enjoy it, too. After all, she had been through so much.

And enjoy it she did. It didn't seem to bother her too much that the family hadn't been invited this time, but I think my being pregnant seemed to take her mind off wider issues, and that worked well. If she was upset by not receiving an invitation from Ken or Bill, she certainly didn't show it, and she didn't say anything to me.

As for Phillip, well Phillip was genuinely pleased with the news that he was going to be a brother. He was adamant about one thing though. He didn't want a sister. I said I would try and oblige.

JANUARY 2002

It was about ten days into the New Year when I received a phone call from Marc. He was warm and pleasant and the phone call was a reminder to me of why I had fallen for him, of why I had loved him and of why I had wanted him to be Phillip's father. The man on the other end of the phone line was someone I remembered, and those memories that stirred in me when I heard his voice, were pleasant ones. It was as though all the recent history, the nastiness, *(that had been there on both sides)* the horrible time of communicating through solicitors had never happened, had never been a significant part of our lives at all. I was relieved.

Part way through the conversation, Marc's voice quietened, became more serious. My stomach sank. I was waiting to hear whatever the bad news was that he had telephoned me to impart. There had to be a reason for an impromptu phone call, there always was. It was never only, *for a chat.*

'... there is a reason why I've phoned. You must have wondered. I hope I've not put you on edge ... or anything ... I ...'

'I'm fine ... you sound ... I was thinking you sound like you used to do ... in the past.'

I didn't know whether I should have said what I had, but that was how I felt. It was good to be speaking to the old Marc. The Marc I had been in love with.

'I've been putting it off, this phone call. I thought that it could wait until the next time I see Phillip, but it can't. It has to be done and now's the best ... there never is a best time for things is there? But, anyway there's something I have to tell you. Is it ok to chat for a little longer now? I promise I won't keep you any longer than I have to, but it's best if there are no interruptions, it's nothing ... oh, this is quite awkward, it'll be easier for me if there are no interruptions.'

'No, nothing will interrupt. I'm here on my own.'

'Good. I thought I should tell you, explain things a little. I never wanted to upset you Christa, never. In fact, I've always loved you, still do actually, and if there was any way we could be together, well, I'd do that for you, too. I'd give anything for that. I hope that doesn't make me sound like a loser, which I know I am in some ways. I lost you after all. Oh, it wasn't meant to be like this, now I'm beginning to sound maudlin.'

'But I don't understand. What is it Marc, what are you trying to say?'

'Just listen, please. I've got to say this and it's not easy for me. I know that what I've just said is pretty much a dream that's dead in the water, and you're happy, I can accept that; and Phillip's happy, that makes things a lot easier for me knowing that my son is happy, and, and I am so pleased that he is my son and that I am his father. You've no idea how happy that makes me, Christa. You're a great mother and knowing that you're going to take care of Phillip, that's worth more than ... well, I know he'll be fine. I want to be part of his life, to visit him, to be a father to him, and that we settled everything, and amicably, was a great relief to me. When I think of how things could have gone, of the mess I could have made of things, it just makes me glad for our friendship. I can say that can't I? We do still have a friendship, don't we?'

I suddenly felt a surge of sadness flow over me. Sadness for this man who was once such a huge part of my life and, what was he trying to tell me? Had I hurt him so much? He had just told me that he loved me. I'd never been able to tell him that, had I? I realised I'd just dried up on the end of the phone. I scrambled my thoughts together.

'Always Marc. We'll always have a friendship. I don't think there's anything that would put paid to that. Not after all we've been through together. And Marc, I'm sorry if you ever thought Phil and I were trying to stop you seeing Phillip, we never were. It was just that Phillip and Jenni didn't seem to get on, they never saw things eye to eye, and well, you know the rest. And Phil and me, we don't have a problem with you visiting him here, and when he gets a little older, a little more self assured, well then things could change again, I'm sure we can sort something out. When you surprised him on his birthday, he was so pleased to see you. I'm sure you could see that. It was the other problems he couldn't deal with, when you phoned him as an inquisitor, not as a father. But that's all done with now, a happy solution reached. And if there's one memory you must never forget, just think back to his birthday, and how pleased he was to see you.'

'Yes, I could see he was pleased. I hoped he would be. I was relieved, actually, that it didn't cause any friction between us.'

'I don't think you should think like that. Phillip is your son, Marc.'

'This getting to the point is taking me longer than I thought it would. Anyway, what I want to tell you, I'm getting a divorce, me and Jenni, we're through; we've already separated.'

'I'm sorry.'

'You needn't be. She wasn't for me, and she was definitely a career woman, first and foremost, and she was good at her work, credit where it's due. But she lied to me when she told me that she couldn't have any more children after she'd miscarried. It was that she didn't want children. It was as simple as that. I think the miscarriage was a blessing in disguise to her, a relief. And to be honest, if we'd had a child it would have been a disaster; we'd still have split up and then our child would have been used as a means to score points off the other parent. It would have been pretty nasty. And not that it would have been her fault but Jenni would have been unable to do the 'mum' bit. It was just never in her nature, sadly.'

'But I thought ...'

'She was a good liar, Christa. She took us all in. Julie's really taken it worse than I thought, but the two of them seemed to be really close. I think Julie will miss Jenni more than I will.'

'I'm sorry Marc, you didn't deserve that. I really am sorry.'

'Is there anyone else involved?' I knew this was really none of my business, but I felt compelled to ask.

'No, not for either of us. We were just ill-matched. I guess you can't love two people at the same time. I don't think Jenni resented what we'd had, Christa, but I'll say that it didn't help in the beginning. She knew I still felt for you, and then ... we just weren't matched. Let's leave it there.'

'I'm sorry. I didn't mean to pry, to dredge up the past. It has nothing to do with me.'

'It has to do with you. Who is it that I have decided to open my heart to?'

'Don't worry about it Marc. I understand, and I'm sorry for you and for Jenni, as well. It must be difficult for her. I'm sure she did love you, you know, she must have done ...'

'Stuck for words, eh?'

'I suppose I am.'

'It's all right you know. There can never be an answer to everything, a response for every situation.'

'Oh if we carry on like this, you'll make me cry, and that's not a good look, believe me. But look, Marc, we've both done things we should have perhaps given more thought to, but Phillip is our son and I never will forget our friendship and what we meant to each other. It means a lot to me, and ... well more than that, I never will forget that I did love you.'

'At last, she says the words I never heard; now, when it's too late.'

And then the phone call ended as politely as it had begun. I pondered what Marc had said and it all seemed a little unreal, and I did feel truly sorry for him.

I talked to Phil about the conversation that I had had with Marc. I couldn't see a problem with what I had said but Phil thought that maybe I was being too pally with the man who had almost broken up our family. I stopped him there. I had too. Phil was the first one to stray, not me, and definitely not Marc. Part of my conversation with Marc I decided to keep to myself. I didn't tell Phil that part of me still loved Marc. I knew that to have mentioned the word *love* in direct relation to Marc would have tipped Phil's reaction against me, and would have only led into a long discussion about the difference between being in love with someone and loving them. I don't think Phil would have understood. I think he would have thought that he was still at risk of losing me, but there was nothing for Phil to worry about, that wasn't going to happen. It had been a difficult conversation, but in the end, Phil agreed with me that as Phillip became older the decisions about whether or not he saw his father would eventually rest on his shoulders. Phil relented, but he wanted things to be on his terms. It seemed that at heart, both these men who played such a large part in my life, were very similar. They were both strong-willed and saw little to justify the other's point of view.

Phillip had his own thoughts on matters, too. He thought that it would be better and easier if Marc came to visit him. He didn't want to do so many trips to London, for special times it would be ok, but not every school holiday. *His friends were all here*, he argued. If he kept going off to London then he would miss a whole weekend of seeing them. I couldn't argue against that one. Phillip was right, another strong-willed male to add to my collection.

One point that Phillip had raised, was that of calling Marc, *dad*. It was the point that had caused so much trouble early on in Phillip's life.

'I know Marc's my dad, and I'd like to call him dad when we meet up and we're out together. It would seem better than calling him Marc ... but everyone, everyone says that I'm just like my dad Phil, and I am, aren't I?'

What could I say? There was no denying it. Phillip and Phil were like two peas in a pod. Phil put a comforting arm around Phillip's shoulder as he spoke.

'I am your dad, you are my son, but as long as you know the truth, I think that Marc will be happy with that. You talk to him about it, man to man and I'm sure he'll be pleased with whatever you decide. It could be Marc or dad, or both. And in a way that makes you really lucky, you've got two dads who think the world of you and who want to look after you and you know that we'll always be here whenever you need us.'

'Yeah, s'pose.' Phillip replied, and then he paused in thought for a moment before adding,

'So you wouldn't mind, if I called Marc 'dad' when he visits me here?'

'Of course I wouldn't mind.'

'Great.'

'No problem,' and Phil hugged Phillip again, to give reassurance.

Phillip's next line of conversation made me smile, although I hope it wasn't too apparent to Phillip.

'So that makes Milly a real half sister?'

'That's right.'

'She's awful sometimes.'

'That's just her now, when you were tiny she looked after you a lot,' I said

'And does this mean that Jenni's another mum?'

'No.' I replied.'No. And Jenni and Marc aren't going to be together from now on. Jenni's done some things and they ...'

Phil interrupted me, which was probably a good thing. There are some things that are best not said. And discussing his father's marriage breakdown with Phillip would have been a bad idea, a step too far. I brought this particular line of the conversation to an end.

'Anyway that's about it Phillip,' I said.

Phillip looked at Phil, and smiled, then said,

'Can we go for a kick about later, dad?'

Phil beamed, 'Yeah, 'course we can.'

APRIL 2002

Our daughter was born safe and well on the twenty-third of April. At thirty-nine, I was considered to be an older mother, which was true and consequently I had been monitored throughout the pregnancy, *'just in case'.* None of that mattered now. Nothing else mattered except that our daughter had arrived safely and that she was perfect and beautiful and everything we could have hoped she'd be. She weighed in at 7lb 6oz, 17" long and cried immediately.

Phil was absolutely over the moon! This was possibly the most delighted I'd ever seen him. I think as time had gone on, we neither of us really felt that we would have a child of our own, but now we had. Now our family and our life was complete. Nothing could touch us. We'd been through so much and had emerged the stronger for it. We'd been tested, and we'd passed that test. I knew that our daughter's birth wouldn't mean that Phillip was pushed out. Phillip was our son and I knew that Phil would always think of him that way. Nothing would change for Phillip; we'd both make sure of that. Phil would never feel any different about Phillip or love him any less; it was just that this time Phil had every right to feel the way he did.

No one could take any part, no matter how small, away from him. This moment, the moment of his daughter's birth, belonged to him as well.

And me? I just wanted to sleep, but as any new mother knows or later will remember, sleep is something that is at a premium in those first few weeks. Thank goodness for the overswell of maternal feelings and joy. Two days after the birth, Phil and Phillip came to collect us, the *'two girls'* from the hospital. I was surprised on arriving back home to see everything looking exactly as I had left it. I think Phillip had been bribed to be tidy and Mum was eager to see us. Phillip had shown her photographs but this was the first time she was seeing our new addition in the flesh. I sat down and got myself comfy, Phil brought out a Moses basket and we placed our new daughter inside. She gurgled and opened one eye, then closed it again and fell fast asleep. Phillip laughed.

'What do you think Mum, of your new granddaughter?' I asked.

I don't know why I bothered asking really. The answer was one to be expected. She just said, 'Perfect, she's perfect.' And of course she was.

To say that Mum was thrilled was an understatement. She was pleased that her daughter and grand-daughter were doing well and safely home.

And Phillip? Well contrary to what Phillip had said before the birth, he didn't seem to mind the fact that he had a little sister.

We named our new daughter Georgia. We were so lucky to have come this far. We both knew that. We also knew that nothing in our lives would ever be left to chance again. Everything we did was to be thought over, talked about and planned. It had taken us a lot of years to get here but what we had was something that was worth looking after, something worth taking care of; and we would never lose sight of that, no matter what.

SEPTEMBER 26th 2010

And now here we are. Back to the present. I've been on my own for most of the day. It is our wedding anniversary. Phil returned from work, came into the kitchen to find me, and then he kissed me, as he always did.

'Had a good day?' he asked.

'Quiet.'

'Ready to go out? I've booked a table. And then there's my gift for you, something silver ...'

He spotted the flowers he'd given me earlier and said, 'They look nice, I know roses are transient, for the moment, but they're beautiful, beautiful like you Chrissy. And the lilies, I picked the lilies you'd had in your bouquet, I think.'

'I know. And they're perfect; but can we just talk for a moment? I have to tell you something. It's been on my mind all day.'

Phil sat down, 'Sounds bad.'

'It is. It's Marc.'

Phil came and drew a chair up to the kitchen table, sat beside me.

'Right. What's happened?

'Julie phoned last night, early hours of this morning. He's had a heart attack, it was sudden. He's dead. Marc's dead.'

'You never said a word before I left this morning. You've been nursing this all day, Chrissy.'

'I didn't want to spoil the day. I thought it could wait, and it has. It's just been so awful. I ... I never expected anything like this.'

I couldn't hold back the tears anymore. Phil held me while I sobbed uncontrollably. Georgia came down the stairs.

'What's up with mummy?'

'She's had bad news love, that's all.' Phil said.

'You're not ill are you, mummy?'

'No Georgia, of course mummy's not ill. I'm doing lots of stuff aren't I, all the mum things.'

Georgia smiled, 'Yes, you are.'

'Well there you are then, there's nothing for you to worry about, but I could do with a cup of tea. Why don't you switch the kettle on? It's already filled with water. When it's boiled I'll make us some tea.'

'Ok.'

As Georgia went through the actions, Phil looked at me.

'Have you spoken to Phillip yet?'

'No, not yet. I thought he'd be in lectures all day. I thought that it'd be best to wait until he was home, back at the flat.'

'Do you want me to do it? He'll have to be told. He'll want to come home, for the funeral.'

'I don't know when that'll be, not yet. Julie's going to let me know, there'll be a post-mortem ... he wasn't ... hadn't been ill, you see.'

I looked up at him.

'Could you call him then, let him know. I'll speak to him ... after you've ...'

Phil took my hand, squeezed it and then hugged me. I needed this comfort from him. It was what I'd needed all day.

'I'll do it later, phone Phillip, about seven, he should be back by then.'

Phil was reliable. He always had been. And in the end that was why I had always loved him.

ABOUT THE AUTHOR

Margaret Holbrook grew up in Cheshire where she still lives. Her work has been published in anthologies and magazines and broadcast on radio.

She writes fiction, plays and poetry.

In 2014 her play *The Supper Party*, was a finalist in the 'Grand Words' competition, run in conjunction with the *Grand Theatre*, Blackpool.

Her short story, *Our Brian*, was longlisted for the BBC Radio 4 programme, 'Opening Lines', in the same year.

In 2015 her play *Sandy's Ashes* was performed at Congleton Festival and in November 2015 her short story *Pig Man* was shortlisted for the Cheshire Prize for Literature, and is published in the Cheshire Prize Anthology, *Patches of Light.*

Website:

www.margaretholbrookwrites.weebly.com

Follow on facebook:

www.facebook.com/soupforstarters